The Prince escorted Vida to the bottom of the stairs, then lifting her hand he held it in both of his before he said:

"Promise you will not disappear during the night back to Olympus, or wherever it is you came from, so that I shall not see you in the morning?"

"I promise."

She laughed as she spoke, then as she looked into the Prince's eyes she found the sound dying away on her lips.

For a moment they just looked at each other, then he bent his handsome head and kissed her hand.

Suddenly afraid of the feelings his kiss evoked within her, she took her hand from his and ran up the staircase without looking back.

THE PERIL AND THE PRINCE

A Camfield Novel of Love

Dearest Reader,

Camfield Novels of Love mark a very exciting era of my books with Jove. They have already published nearly two hundred of my titles since they became my first publisher in America, and now all my original paperback romances in the future will be published exclusively by them.

As you already know, Camfield Place in Hertfordshire is my home, which originally existed in 1275, but was rebuilt in 1867 by the grandfather of Beatrix Potter.

It was here in this lovely house, with the best view in the county, that she wrote *The Tale of Peter Rabbit*. Mr. McGregor's garden is exactly as she described it. The door in the wall that the fat little rabbit could not squeeze underneath and the goldfish pool where the white cat sat twitching its tail are still there.

I had Camfield Place blessed when I came here in 1950 and was so happy with my husband until he died, and now with my children and grandchildren, that I know the atmosphere is filled with love and we have all been very lucky.

It is easy here to write of love and I know you will enjoy the Camfield Novels of Love. Their plots are definitely exciting and the covers very romantic. They come to you, like all my books, with love.

Bless you,

CAMFIELD NOVELS OF LOVE
by Barbara Cartland

THE POOR GOVERNESS
WINGED VICTORY
LUCKY IN LOVE
LOVE AND THE MARQUIS
A MIRACLE IN MUSIC
LIGHT OF THE GODS
BRIDE TO A BRIGAND
LOVE COMES WEST

A WITCH'S SPELL
SECRETS
THE STORMS OF LOVE
MOONLIGHT ON THE
    SPHINX
WHITE LILAC
REVENGE OF THE HEART
THE ISLAND OF LOVE

THERESA AND A TIGER
LOVE IS HEAVEN
MIRACLE FOR A
    MADONNA
A VERY UNUSUAL WIFE
THE PERIL AND THE
    PRINCE

Other books by Barbara Cartland

THE ADVENTURER
AGAIN THIS RAPTURE
BARBARA CARTLAND'S
    BOOK OF BEAUTY
    AND HEALTH
BLUE HEATHER
BROKEN BARRIERS
THE CAPTIVE HEART
THE COIN OF LOVE
THE COMPLACENT WIFE
COUNT THE STARS
CUPID RIDES PILLION
DANCE ON MY HEART
DESIRE OF THE HEART
DESPERATE DEFIANCE
THE DREAM WITHIN
A DUEL OF HEARTS
ELIZABETHAN LOVER
THE ENCHANTING EVIL
ESCAPE FROM PASSION
FOR ALL ETERNITY
A GHOST IN MONTE
    CARLO
THE GOLDEN GONDOLA
A HALO FOR THE DEVIL
A HAZARD OF HEARTS
A HEART IS BROKEN
THE HEART OF THE
    CLAN
THE HIDDEN EVIL
THE HIDDEN HEART
THE HORIZONS OF LOVE
IN THE ARMS OF LOVE

THE IRRESISTIBLE BUCK
THE KISS OF PARIS
THE KISS OF THE DEVIL
A KISS OF SILK
THE KNAVE OF HEARTS
THE LEAPING FLAME
A LIGHT TO THE HEART
LIGHTS OF LOVE
THE LITTLE PRETENDER
LOST ENCHANTMENT
LOST LOVE
LOVE AND LINDA
LOVE AT FORTY
LOVE FORBIDDEN
LOVE IN HIDING
LOVE IN PITY
LOVE IS AN EAGLE
LOVE IS CONTRABAND
LOVE IS DANGEROUS
LOVE IS MINE
LOVE IS THE ENEMY
LOVE ME FOREVER
LOVE ON THE RUN
LOVE TO THE RESCUE
LOVE UNDER FIRE
THE MAGIC OF HONEY
MESSENGER OF LOVE
METTERNICH: THE
    PASSIONATE
    DIPLOMAT
MONEY, MAGIC AND
    MARRIAGE
NO HEART IS FREE

THE ODIOUS DUKE
OPEN WINGS
OUT OF REACH
THE PRICE IS LOVE
A RAINBOW TO HEAVEN
THE RELUCTANT BRIDE
THE RUNAWAY
    HEART
THE SCANDALOUS LIFE
    OF KING CAROL
THE SECRET FEAR
THE SMUGGLED HEART
A SONG OF LOVE
STARS IN MY HEART
STOLEN HALO
SWEET ADVENTURE
SWEET ENCHANTRESS
SWEET PUNISHMENT
THEFT OF A HEART
THE THIEF OF LOVE
THIS TIME IT'S LOVE
TOUCH A STAR
TOWARDS THE STARS
THE UNKNOWN HEART
THE UNPREDICTABLE
    BRIDE
A VIRGIN IN PARIS
WE DANCED ALL NIGHT
WHERE IS LOVE?
THE WINGS OF ECSTASY
THE WINGS OF LOVE
WINGS ON MY HEART
WOMAN, THE ENIGMA

A NEW CAMFIELD NOVEL OF LOVE BY

BARBARA CARTLAND

The Peril and the Prince

A JOVE BOOK

THE PERIL AND THE PRINCE

A Jove Book/published by arrangement with
the author

PRINTING HISTORY
Jove edition/April 1985

ISBN: 0-515-08171-X

Jove books are published by The Berkley Publishing Group,
200 Madison Avenue, New York, N.Y. 10016.
The words "A JOVE BOOK" and the "J" with sunburst
are trademarks belonging to Jove Publications, Inc.

PRINTED IN THE UNITED STATES OF AMERICA

AUTHOR'S NOTE

THE descriptions of Tzar Alexander III, 1881–1894, are all correct and he was in fact one of the most unpleasant and cruel rulers Russia ever had.

His first act on becoming Emperor was to tear up the unsigned manifesto lying on his father's death-bed which made provision for a limited form of representative government at a national level.

The Tzar opened his reign with a persecution of the Jews which was to be unequalled until the event, fifty years later, of Adolf Hitler in Germany.

It was proclaimed that one-third of all the Jews in Russia must die, one third emigrate, and one third assimilate.

The Tzar wore his clothes until they were thread-bare, his children were often hungry, and he reduced his Civil List by down-ranking the nobles. It is not surprising that mediaeval gloom hung over the Court.

The Secret Police instigated by Nicholas I and known as The Third Section, terrified the whole country. They were ruthless, corrupt, and savagely cruel.

chapter one
1887

THE Clerk knocked tentatively on the door of the Secretary of State for Foreign Affairs. There was a pause before the Marquess of Salisbury replied.

"Come in."

He was writing at his large, flat-topped desk and did not look up for some seconds while the Clerk stood somewhat uncomfortably at the doorway.

"What is it?"

"I am sorry to disturb Your Lordship, but there is a young lady here who insists on seeing you."

"A young lady?"

"Her name, My Lord, is Miss Anstruther."

For a moment the Marquess looked blank and then he said:

"I wonder . . . ? Show her in."

"Very good, My Lord."

The Clerk shut the door quietly and returned a few minutes later to announce:

"Miss Vida Anstruther, My Lord."

The Marquess rose slowly to his feet as his visitor came towards him.

She looked very young, but her composure and self-confidence made him think she was very likely older.

She was certainly very lovely and as he held out his hand he said:

"I think you must be the daughter of Sir Harvey Anstruther."

She smiled and it was as if sunshine suddenly filled the rather gloomy office.

"I have come to talk to you about him."

"I rather suspected that," the Marquess said. "Will you sit down."

He indicated an upright chair on the other side of his desk and she seated herself slowly and without the indecision that he expected from a girl.

The Marquess of Salisbury, who was also the Prime Minister, was in fact a very intimidating man. Even his colleagues in the House of Lords looked on him with awe.

He was also extremely clever and he knew he had the full confidence of the Queen as well as the Cabinet.

"What I have come to ask you, My Lord," Vida Anstruther began, and now there was undoubtedly a worried note in her soft voice, "is what has happened to my father?"

"It is a question I have been asking myself since I received a report a few weeks ago that he was missing," the Marquess replied. "But I am quite certain, considering where he is, it is too soon for you to worry about him."

"That is where you are wrong, My Lord," Vida

Anstruther contradicted. "I am, in fact, extremely worried, for while it is only in the last few weeks that you have heard my father is missing, I have not heard from him for nearly two months."

The Marquess leant back in his chair and said in a serious tone:

"As long as that? I am surprised you did not communicate with me before."

"I did not do so because, as you know, Papa dislikes very much being interfered with when he is travelling more or less incognito."

She paused and then went on.

"But I expect you know why he went to Hungary. The reason he gave to his friends was that he was visiting my mother's family, and he was taking a holiday after so many strenuous years in the service of his country."

"Of course I understand," the Marquess said, "and that was exactly what your father told me he would say before he left."

Vida Anstruther did not speak and he continued.

"What I suspect has happened is that he crossed into Russia, which is what he intended to do, and is either on the track of something of great importance and therefore will not return immediately, or else he has decided to go south to Odessa and come home by a different route from the one he took on his outward journey."

"That sounds very plausible, My Lord," Vida Anstruther replied, "but I am quite certain that Papa is in danger!"

She thought the Marquess looked sceptical and she said:

"You may think it strange, but because Papa and

I have been so close to each other since Mama died, we each know what the other is thinking. My sixth sense, if that is what you like to call it, tells me that either the Russians have arrested him or else he is in hiding and finding it impossible to return home."

"I can understand your feelings," the Marquess said after a moment, "but what you are saying is entirely supposition and you have no genuine foundation for such ideas."

"Only my conviction that what has undeniably saved my father's life many times in the past has been his instinct."

There was silence. Then as if the Marquess was convinced by the certainty with which his visitor spoke he said after a moment:

"I think you must be aware, Miss Anstruther, that even if you are right there is nothing I can do about it."

"I know that, and that is why I am going to do something myself."

The Marquess stiffened.

"I hope you are not speaking seriously."

"I am very serious. I intend to try to find Papa and I need your help."

"If you are thinking of going out to Hungary and from there into Russia, I can only say it would be an extremely foolhardy action of which I know your father would disapprove. I shall try my very best to make you change your mind."

"You will not be able to do so, My Lord," Vida Anstruther replied, and now there was a touch of steel in her voice. "I have thought it out carefully, and what I intend is to tell everyone that I am going out to join

Papa in Hungary and that we had arranged that before he left."

She looked at the Marquess as if she were challenging him. He did not speak and she went on.

"All I need from Your Lordship is a passport with a false name under which I shall travel. It would be very stupid, if I am right in thinking Papa is in danger, to be known as his daughter once I have left these shores."

The Marquess knew this was common sense, but he had no intention of giving in so easily.

"Let me make a suggestion, Miss Anstruther," he said. "I will send one of my most trusted men to look for your father. I have already had reports that he arrived safely in Hungary, and was received by your mother's family with enthusiasm."

"And what did you hear after that?"

"I was told that your father had gone on a hunting expedition which might or might not have carried him into Russia, but he had not returned and there was a certain amount of anxiety as to what might have happened to him."

Vida Anstruther's eyes were stormy as she asked:

"And you were content with that report?"

"Of course I was not content with it," the Marquess replied, "but there can be many reasons for your father's disappearance. The last thing he would want is for anyone to go looking for him and perhaps reveal his identity. That could prove embarrassing and might even endanger his life."

He spoke sharply because he told himself that the young girl facing him had no idea of the difficulties her father might be encountering or what damage might be done by inexperienced handling of the situation.

Vida Anstruther merely said in much the same tone as the Marquess had used to her:

"Of course I am well aware of what you are saying. You forget that I have been with Papa for the last five years in all sorts of strange places and at times in very uncomfortable circumstances. That is why you can trust me not to do anything foolish or what you would call unprofessional when I go to look for him."

The way she spoke made the Marquess feel although it seemed ridiculous, that he ought to apologise, and after a moment he said:

"I must admit, Miss Anstruther, I was not aware how close you were to your father. In fact, I had supposed that when he went 'travelling,' as one might say, you were left behind in whatever Embassy he was posted at that time."

"I never allowed Papa to go alone," Vida Anstruther replied, "and I can assure you he found me very useful. When I was younger, people usually did not think it mattered what they said in front of a child, and later he found that since I am as good at languages as he is himself, I could often pass on to him information which was extremely useful."

The Marquess thought with a glint of amusement in his eyes that if Miss Anstruther had acted as a spy, which was what she was implying, she was certainly a very attractive one.

It was a pity the Foreign Office could not make use of her!

But he knew it was his duty to dissuade her from getting mixed up in what he was well aware was a very tricky situation.

The Russian Tzar had, for some time, been behaving in a manner described by Queen Victoria as "shamefully."

Alexander III was an unpredictable and an extremely unpleasant Ruler. He liked to play the part of a simple-minded muzhik, but he had a strong streak of Asiatic cunning in his make-up.

He locked up all revolutionaries at home, but encouraged them abroad.

He was in fact, although no-one realised it at the time, the first leader in history of a great country to wage an organised "cold war."

He had Russians stirring up trouble for the regimes established in the Balkans by the Treaty of Berlin in 1878; Russian under-cover men posing as Icon-sellers wandering through Serbia setting up subversive cells; Russian Embassy officials paying crowds to stage riots.

In Bulgaria Russians had actually kidnapped Prince Alexander of Battenberg and forced him to abdicate at pistol-point.

The outcry in Europe had been stupendous, but the new ruler of Bulgaria, Prince Ferdinand of Coburg, was supported by a staunch patriot, Stambulov, who was just as hostile to Russia as the former Government had been.

Russian agents were therefore at the moment concentrating on murdering him.

What concerned Britain even more closely than what was happening in Europe was that the Tzar's armies were moving steadily outwards in Asia and by infiltrating into Afghanistan were menacing India.

Reliable information was very scarce from that isolated country, but Sir Harvey Anstruther had volunteered to try to find out what was happening within Russia itself.

He had the perfect excuse of visiting his former wife's relatives, who lived in the Eastern part of Hungary, very close to the frontier with Russia.

"Some of your mother's cousins have, I know, married Russians," Sir Harvey had said to Vida before he left, "and I may learn something from them. I am, moreover, quite certain I shall hear a great deal from the Hungarian families in the neighbourhood who, unless they have changed a great deal in the past few years, have always disliked the Russians and mistrusted them."

Vida had smiled.

She was only too well aware of how patriotic the Hungarians were, and how they disapproved of the manner in which the Russian aristocrats treated their serfs and of the systematic terrorism which was an integral part of Russian rule.

She had wanted to go with her father but he had dissuaded her.

"I have arranged for the Duchess of Dorset to present you at one of the first Drawing Rooms," he had said, "and it would not only be rude if you cried off but might lead to a lot of awkward questions as to why I am going so far afield."

He had smiled before he added:

"I shall not be away long, my dearest, and when I return I expect to find you the Belle of the Season, and although it is something I would deplore, the acknowledged toast of St. James's."

She had given in to him because she knew how anxious he was that she should take her proper place in Society.

At the same time, when he had finally left on a cold, windy day at the beginning of February, she had put her arms round his neck and said:

"Promise me you will take care of yourself, Papa. You know how much you mean to me. I cannot lose you!"

"I will be careful for your sake," her father had replied, "and to me you mean everything in the whole world."

'I knew then that it was wrong for him to go,' Vida had thought to herself later.

But by then it was too late, and while her father was speeding across Europe she was choosing the clothes in which she was to make her début.

She was actually almost too old to be a débutante, being nineteen on her next birthday, which was in two weeks time.

But last year, which would have been the appropriate time for her to be presented, her father had been Ambassador in Vienna, which the Foreign Office considered a post of considerable importance and would not hear of his returning.

Vida had therefore stayed with him, and it was only now, when he had asked for a long leave of absence before he took over the Embassy in Paris, that he had been asked to undertake a very special mission.

"Why can they not leave you alone, Papa?" Vida had asked angrily. "You have done so much for them and, as far as I can ascertain, got little thanks for it."

"I do not want thanks," her father had said quietly. "Whatever I do is to help my country where and when she most needs it, and I cannot pretend with mock modesty that I do not have the qualifications for such a mission."

He did not add that there was nobody who even

nearly equalled him in his remarkable proficiency in mastering foreign languages.

Also high ranking as he was, he enjoyed assuming disguises when need arose, in a way no other Ambassador of his standing would think of doing.

However because he was a very exceptional person, Sir Harvey thought such behaviour a great joke.

He would make his daughter laugh helplessly at stories of how he had haggled as a carpet-seller or a Bedouin guide with distinguished personages with whom he had been at school or University without their having the slightest idea of who he was.

Before leaving for Hungary he had said lightheartedly that for the first time in years he would be travelling as himself and therefore expecting to enjoy the red carpet and all the comforts and privileges of his Diplomatic rank.

Vida had, however, known that he was trying to pull the wool over her eyes.

She was quite certain that after reaching Hungary he would cross the border either purporting to be a Russian or in some other subtle disguise which even the most astute of the Tzar's Secret Police would be unable to penetrate.

Then two months ago she had suddenly become aware that things were very different from what Sir Harvey had told her to expect.

It was impossible to convince the Marquess of Salisbury that she had an almost clairvoyant awareness of anything that concerned her father.

She was coming away from the Drawing Room at Buckingham Palace when she had what she knew for certain was a warning that her father was in danger.

She had just come down the red-carpeted stairs from the Throne Room and was stepping into the carriage that was waiting outside.

Bending her head low because she was wearing the traditional three Prince of Wales's white ostrich feathers on top of her head, she felt as if an icy hand gripped her heart.

For a moment she thought it might be the effect of the glass of champagne she had sipped after making her curtsy to the Queen and the Prince and Princess of Wales.

Then she knew it was something very different and she was frightened.

She felt almost as if her father were actually speaking to her.

As she thought of him and concentrated in the manner that he had taught her to do, she was so still and silent that as the carriage proceeded along the Mall and turned up St. James's Street, the Duchess said:

"Are you all right? I hope you are not going to faint. It was very hot and airless in the Throne Room."

"No, I am all right, thank you," Vida answered, but she knew at the same time that she lied.

She was suddenly desperately afraid for her father and what was happening to him.

Now looking across the desk at the Marquess of Salisbury, she said firmly:

"All I am asking, My Lord, is that you should arrange for me a passport in a new name I shall assume once I am out of the country."

She thought he was hesitating and she said:

"I do not wish to threaten you, My Lord, but as

11

you must be well aware, false passports are not impossible to obtain. However, I would rather come to you than put myself in the hands of people whom it would be impossible to trust seeing they are already behaving illegally."

"No. No, of course not!" the Marquess said. "That would be an extremely foolish thing to do."

"That is why I am asking for your co-operation."

As if he realised that nothing he said to her would divert her from doing what she intended, the Marquess after a considerable pause said grudgingly:

"Very well. You make it difficult for me to refuse you, though it is something I am sure I ought to do."

He pulled a piece of paper towards him and asked:

"What name do you wish to use?"

As Vida had thought this out carefully before she had come to the Foreign Office she said:

"Countess Vida Kărólzi."

The Marquess's eyebrows went up.

"Russian?"

"That might be useful, and at the same time it is a name that might easily be Hungarian if you put the accents in the right places."

The Marquess laughed because he could not help it.

"Before you ask me," Vida went on, "I am keeping my own Christian name because not only does it sound foreign, which it is, but Papa's advice has always been 'never tell a lie if you can possibly help it.'"

The Marquess had to laugh again.

"I can only say you are incorrigible, Miss Anstruther, and although you are persuading me to do something of which I very much disapprove, I cannot

12

really think how I can stop you."

"That is not surprising," Vida said, "since I have every intention of going to find Papa. It would also be useful if in an emergency I could know if there are any of your own men in reach of where I shall be who could help me."

Again the Marquess hesitated before he wrote down a name on a piece of paper in front of him and handed it across the desk.

"As your father's daughter," he said, "you are well aware that the life of this man is in your hands. Commit his name to memory and then destroy this paper, and promise me that only in an emergency which affects the life of you or your father you will call upon him."

"I promise you that I will be as careful as my father would be in the same circumstances."

"That is all I ask," the Marquess replied. "And now we will do what we can about your passport."

He rang a bell attached to his desk as he spoke and when the door opened he said:

"Ask Mr. Tritton to come to me."

Mr. Tritton was, as Vida was not surprised to see, a middle-aged man with a worried look on his face, which came, she was sure, from being burdened with secrets that must never be disclosed outside the Foreign Office.

The Marquess handed him the piece of paper on which he had written the name Vida had chosen for her passport and then as the door closed behind him he said:

"I expect you would wish to take it with you as it would be wise not to make too many visits here. We never know who is watching our doors."

"That is what I thought," Vida replied, "and I can only say I am very grateful for your help, My Lord."

"Given very reluctantly!"

She smiled at him and he thought that she was not only lovely but very unlike any British girl of her age.

"I know your mother was Hungarian," he said. "Did you ever visit her family when your father was in Vienna?"

Vida shook her head.

"There never seemed to be time," she answered, "but some of my relatives, only the younger ones, came to see us in Vienna. Those who were older had no wish to travel."

"And you say you are as proficient at languages as your father?"

"He has taught me everything he knows," Vida replied. "At the same time it has been useful having a Russian grandmother."

The Marquess sat upright.

"I had no idea of that."

"She was dead before I was born so I never met her," Vida said, "but as Russian is the most difficult language in the world to learn, with the exception perhaps of Chinese, it has been of inestimable benefit to be able to speak it almost naturally and in fact not find it at all difficult."

"That indeed is an almost incredible asset," the Marquess said. "But let me beg you, Miss Anstruther, not to do anything foolhardy, such as going to Russia unless it is to make the same sort of friendly visit you would make in any other country."

He paused while choosing his words and then said:

"As you are of course aware, there is a great deal

of animosity between us and the Tzar at the present moment. I am not disclosing any secrets when I say that we have nearly come to war over Afghanistan, and I am quite certain the Tzar has little or no goodwill towards the English."

"Papa was sure that he was in fact furious, because his forces have not been successful in infiltrating into India, not even into the North-West Provinces."

The Marquess did not reply, and Vida was sure he felt it would be indiscreet to discuss it with her.

Tactfully she said:

"Is there anyone that would be useful for me to get in touch with either in Hungary or just over the frontier?"

As she spoke she knew she was reading the Marquess's mind, and that he was thinking of someone although he had not intended to reveal it to her.

But now he looked penetratingly at her across the desk, and she was aware that he was wondering whether or not he could trust her.

"Please," she said, "I swear to you on all I hold holy, I know that Papa is in danger."

The sincerity with which she spoke helped the Marquess to make up his mind.

"Very well," he said. "I will tell you about one man who is I believe of vital importance, although the information I have about him is very varied."

"Who is he?"

"His name is Prince Ivan Pavolivski."

Vida was listening intently as the Marquess went on.

"He is a strange, enigmatic man who may be all that he pretends."

"What is that?"

"Like many of the Russian nobility, he comes to Western Europe for amusement and spends some time every year in Monte Carlo, where he has a villa, as have the Grand Duke Boris and the Grand Duke Michael. He is also well-known in Paris, and made a visit last year to London."

Vida knew that this was nothing unusual, and the Russian aristocrats with their enormous wealth and generous hospitality were welcome everywhere.

"What is different about Prince Ivan," the Marquess went on, "is that no-one is quite certain where his allegiance lies."

Vida looked puzzled and he explained.

"He has many friends in Hungary who find him a great sportsman and enthusiastically welcome his social visits. But from reports I have received, although I admit they are scanty, he is also *persona grata* with the Tzar which, from our point of view, makes him an object of suspicion."

"So you think he is not entirely a playboy?" Vida asked.

"I am quite certain he is far too intelligent not to understand everything that takes place around him, and he may be deeply involved in politics."

The Marquess made a sudden gesture of concession with his hands.

"I admit that when I met him I found him an enigma. He may be just what on the surface he appears to be or he may be at the very centre of the plots we are trying to anticipate and the puzzles we are trying to unravel. I just do not know."

Vida drew in her breath.

"Thank you," she said. "Perhaps the Prince will

be able to tell me about Papa."

The Marquess held up his hands.

"For God's sake, do not trust him unless you feel absolutely certain you can do so."

Then he added in a worried tone:

"Perhaps I should not have told you about the Prince. He has the reputation since he is so handsome of being irresistible to women. If you are carried away by his charm, as undoubtedly many women have been, you might inadvertently be writing your father's death-warrant."

"I am not a fool, My Lord," Vida said coldly, "and I can assure you after your warning that if I do approach the Prince I shall be on my guard and I will do nothing that could in any way endanger Papa's life or that of anyone else in your service."

She spoke with a seriousness that made the Marquess simply say:

"Thank you."

As he spoke the door opened and Mr. Tritton returned with the passport.

Vida put it quickly into her bag, and then as soon as she was alone with the Marquess again she rose to her feet saying:

"I can only say thank-you from the bottom of my heart! The moment Papa and I are safe we will communicate with you."

"Your father knows how to do that without anyone being able to understand what he is saying."

"Yes, I know," Vida said.

"I am not certain whether I should approve or disapprove of Sir Harvey confiding in you," the Marquess replied.

"I can assure you that Papa and I have always worked together as a team," Vida answered, "and I know now that I should have gone with him on this journey. I had not realised that anything could be so time-wasting and irrelevant as attending the Drawing Room at Buckingham Palace."

She spoke in an almost scathing manner, which made the Marquess look at her curiously.

He knew that for most young women it was the golden moment in their lives, a privilege they would never forget. But Vida Anstruther was holding out her hand to him and as he took it in his hand he said:

"I can only beg you, my dear, to take care of yourself. You are too young and much too pretty to get involved in what I often think is a very unpleasant mess."

"At the same time, My Lord," Vida answered, "you must admit it is far more exciting and rewarding than attending tea-parties or dancing with inane young men whose only topic of conversation is which horse is going to win at Ascot."

She spoke with a sarcastic note in her voice and looked so lovely as she did so that the Marquess could only laugh.

"You are undermining the whole foundations of English social life, Miss Anstruther," he said as he walked with her to the door.

"I should hate to do that," she replied. "At the same time I have the feeling, although I may be wrong, that it is only a question of time before it is as dead as the dodo."

The Marquess had no answer to this and he could only think as he returned to his desk that he had just conducted a very strange interview and hoped that he had not done the wrong thing.

Vida, however, as she stepped into the comfortable closed brougham that was waiting for her outside, was thinking excitedly that she had got her own way and would be able to leave tomorrow on her journey to find her father.

She had been half afraid that the Marquess would refuse point-blank to give her the passport she required.

This would have necessitated her going to a certain rather unsavoury basement in the Strand where there was a man who had once served five years in prison for forgery.

He could, she knew, produce a faked passport that even the most astute official would find it hard to detect.

Such things, however, always took time besides costing a great deal of money.

She was glad she had been sensible enough to start at the top with the Marquess.

She patted her handbag with a gesture of satisfaction to think that she had with her what she hoped was a passport both to a journey of discovery and to the salvation of her father.

She had of course not gone to the Foreign Office alone, for seated opposite her inside the brougham was a very conventional elderly housemaid, who had been ordered by the Duchess of Dorset to look after her while she was staying in the house.

The Duchess, who was a distant relative of her father, had consented to present Vida at Court and to introduce her to the Social world.

Although ostensibly it was all in the name of friend-ship, Vida was aware her father had paid a very large bill for the Duchess's gowns as well as for her own, and had met the expenses of a Ball which had been held the previous week at the Duchess's house.

He had also provided the horses which were pulling the brougham and were very superior animals to any-thing in the Duke's stables.

It was extremely fortunate that Sir Harvey had not only inherited a considerable fortune from his father, but had also been clever enough to invest it on the best advice.

This had resulted in his doubling his wealth over the last four years.

He was in fact rich enough to retire at any moment he wished to do so and live the life of a country gentleman, enjoying nothing more thrilling than seeing his racing-colours pass the winning-post first in every Classic race.

Yet apart from the fact that he had always wished to crown his career by being appointed to British Am-bassador in Paris, Sir Harvey had all through his life almost deliberately sought danger.

He had found it impossible to remain inactive and allow the enemies of Great Britain to flourish because the British themselves were not astute enough to dis-cover them.

"It is not soldiers and sailors of whom we have to be afraid, my dear," he had often said to Vida. "They openly proclaim their allegiance."

"Those who are dangerous," Sir Harvey continued slowly, "are the snakes who twist themselves into the confidence of the nation's rulers; the chameleons who change there colour with the world opinion; the wolves wearing sheep's clothing who enjoy shedding blood without incurring any danger themselves."

He had spoken so violently that Vida had been surprised.

But as she grew older and learnt of the political intrigues that went on in every country in Europe and Asia, she knew her father was right in saying it was those who worked in disguise or underground who were a menace of which ordinary decent men were totally unaware.

She knew it thrilled Sir Harvey as nothing else was able to do when he succeeded in exposing and bringing their just deserts to men who were undermining the power of Britain.

They all too often were involved in blackmailing or collaborating with British people themselves.

"I will expose them if it is the last thing I do," she had heard her father say.

The amazing thing was that he himself had managed to remain unsuspected by the enemy, and so was successful.

But she knew in the back of her mind there was always fear that one day he would be discovered, and she could not believe that he was not already, although he laughed at the idea, a marked man.

Then she told herself to be afraid was to make oneself vulnerable before going into battle.

'I have to believe, as Papa always does, that I shall win,' she thought.

She braced herself as the carriage drew near to the Duchess's house, for the scene there would inevitably be when she informed her hostess she was leaving the next morning for France.

The Duchess was not only furious but affronted.

"How can you be so ridiculous?" she asked. "You have been a success overnight. There are no less than thirty-four invitations, my secretary tells me, waiting to be answered!"

"I am sorry, Cousin Alice," Vida said, "but I promised Mama's relatives that I would go to stay with them in the summer, and I had no idea that you would be so kind or that you would not have grown tired of me by this time."

"You can go later," the Duchess said firmly.

Vida shook her head.

"I think that would be very rude when they have been expecting me for so long, and have made a great many preparations to entertain me."

She paused and then added as if she were playing the trump card:

"And of course, Papa is waiting to come back with me so that I shall not travel alone. He will be very angry if I keep him waiting when he has so much to do here in England."

"It is very inconsiderate of your father!" the Duchess retorted crossly. "He should have thought of all this before he went gallivanting off to Hungary."

She paused and added indignantly:

"Personally I think he should have been here with you and come with us to Buckingham Palace. I know that the Prince of Wales has a very soft spot for him. In fact, His Royal Highness asked me how he was and when he was likely to see him again."

"I am sure that will be very soon," Vida replied, and prayed it would be.

Only when she had finally got her own way and was driving from Dorset House towards Victoria Station did she think with a leap of her heart that every-thing had gone far better than she had expected.

The Duchess had made a fuss about her travelling alone until Vida explained she was doing nothing of the sort.

She was taking with her not only a Courier of whom her father had always approved, but also an elderly lady's-maid who had been with her at the Embassy in Vienna and who was so experienced a traveller that as Vida said lightly:

"Margit could easily find her way to the moon!"

Margit was in fact not English, but half Austrian and half French with a Greek grandmother, which made her proficient in a great number of languages.

She was over fifty but had found London dull, although she had enjoyed the prestige of staying with the Duchess.

"The servants are all like morons!" she had said in Hungarian to Vida so that they would not be under-stood. "They think only of drinking tea and fighting for their rightful place at the table."

Vida had laughed.

"That is England for you! Protocol here is far more strict than in any Embassy in which we have lived."

"So I have found," Margit had said gloomily. "And because I am a foreigner they kept talking to me as if I were an imbecile."

"The English are very insular," Vida remarked, and Margit snorted.

Vida thought that one blessing about the old maid was that she did not mind setting off even on a long journey, which most women of her age would have found too arduous.

In fact, as soon as they crossed the Channel Margit seemed to get younger and started her invariable fight to get the best carriage and the best sleeper on the Express while demanding every attention which a seasoned traveller expects from the attendant.

With Margit being as fierce as a tigress in caring for her cub and with plenty of money to tip, Vida knew that she would certainly suffer no hardships on the journey.

Actually she was just as excited as Margit was.

It was only after they had passed through France and Germany and were already half-way across into Hungary that she called both Margit and the Courier into her compartment.

"I have something to say to you both," she said in a quiet voice, "and it is very important that from now on we do not make any mistakes."

"Now what're you up to, Miss?" Margit asked in the familiar tone of an old servant who found it hard to remember that Vida was not a child.

"What I am up to," Vida replied, "is that from this moment I am no longer Miss Anstruther. In fact we have never heard of Sir Harvey Anstruther nor of Mama's relations."

"Are you telling me, Miss Vida," Margit asked, "that we're not going to stay at your mother's castle?"

"No, we are not," Vida said. "I am the Comtesse Vida Kárólzi and I am on my way to Sarospatak."

As she spoke she realised that Margit and the Courier were listening intently.

They had travelled with her and her father before, and they were both well aware that Sir Harvey was not always exactly what he appeared to be to the general public.

It was however something new for Vida to do something on her own, and she was aware that Margit automatically disapproved even though she did not say anything.

"We will of course travel by train as far as it is possible," she said, "but once we reach Sarospatak I expect we will have to take a carriage and horses, and I will tell you then exactly where I wish to go."

She looked at the Courier as she spoke and he said in a resigned voice:

"I hope, Miss Vida, you'll not do anything dangerous. I feel responsible for you to your father."

"My father, unfortunately, is dead," Vida said. "He was a Russian who spent his life, ever since I was born in Europe, travelling from one great city to another, preferring Paris since being a widower he found the gaieties there very enjoyable."

She paused before she continued slowly.

"I have of course always longed to see my homeland, which is in the south of Russia, but this has been the first opportunity I have had of doing so."

She smiled at the rather tense faces of the two people listening to her before she went on.

"I am aged twenty-three and I am the widow of a very distinguished Frenchman who was killed in a duel. I have however reverted to my maiden name and I am trying to forget my unhappiness by travelling."

There was silence as she stopped speaking before she added:

"Those are the bare bones of my life and of course we can add flesh to them as we go along. I do not need to add that we must all stick to the same story."

"Of course, M'Lady," the Courier agreed.

He spoke in Russian and Vida laughed.

"You are quite right, Henri," she said. "As a Kă-rólzi I must polish up my Russian. From now on we will talk no other language, and that goes for you too, Margit."

"I dislike Russian, and I'm not good at it," Margit said sulkily.

"Well, you will just have to learn to be better," Vida said unfeelingly. "Now, Henri, go and change the labels on my luggage. If the guard is aware of it, tip him generously so that he will not talk. And you, Margit, must square the attendant.

Her eyes were troubled at the expression on Margit's face as she said:

"You had best tell him, as he knows me as Miss Anstruther, that I married the Count Kărólzi secretly, and am now going to join him in his own country."

"Lies, lies. All we have in this life is lies!" Margit said. "I can't think what Her Grace would say if she knew what you were doing."

"As she is not likely to know," Vida replied logically, "there is no point in our worrying about her feelings in the matter. I do not need to tell either of you what this whole journey is about. The fact is I am afraid that something has happened to Papa."

The expression in her eyes, as much as the way she spoke, made both of the elderly servants look at her sympathetically.

They were aware that Sir Harvey was overdue on a trip from which he should have returned weeks ago.

"Now, don't you go upsettin' yourself," Margit said. "It'll do no good, and when you find your father merely enjoying himself you'll have lines under your eyes for nothing."

The way she spoke made Vida laugh even though there was a touch of tears in the sound, and she said softly:

"Thank you both. You know I could not do this without you, and all that matters is that we should be successful."

chapter two

BUDAPEST was the terminus for the Express Train on which they had come from France, and there they would have to change.

It had been a long journey, but for Vida quite a comfortable one. Shortly before reaching Budapest, in order to match her new name, Vida altered her appearance.

Margit packed away the simple travelling-gowns she had worn since leaving London.

Instead, Vida put on a far more elaborate creation which she had bought deliberately together with a great many other more sophisticated clothes before calling on the Prime Minister.

She also, in foreign fashion, used cosmetics on her face, which she thought swept away the last trace of an English appearance.

It certainly made her look older and in a way much more attractive, but she was concerned only with entering into her new personality.

She remembered her father had said the most important part of a disguise was to "think" yourself into the part.

Then you would be convincing enough for people to believe you were what you pretended to be.

They had some time to wait at Budapest before catching a much slower train which would carry them farther eastwards through Hungary.

There was a restaurant at the station which was divided into an expensive section for important travellers and a much cheaper one for those who could not afford to pay much for their food.

The more exclusive part was shielded by ferns and pots of flowers from the other and had white cloths on the tables and padded chairs on which to sit.

Vida was shown to what she thought was the best table and ordered herself quite a large meal with half a bottle of the best local wine.

The waiters were extremely attentive.

There were only two or three other people eating in the same room with plenty of available tables, so she was surprised when a well-dressed man came up to her and said:

"I hope, Madame, you will permit me to sit at your table."

She looked at him and realised that he appeared to be a gentleman, although there was something about him she could not place.

After a moment's pause she replied to his question:

"I cannot, of course, Monsieur, prevent you from

sitting anywhere you wish, but I am in fact, enjoying my meal alone."

"I do not believe that," he said in a somewhat flirtatious tone, and pulling out a chair sat down beside her.

"You must forgive my curiosity," he said after a moment, "but you do not look entirely Hungarian and I am trying to place you."

"I cannot think why," Vida replied.

They were talking Hungarian and yet listening intently she had the idea, though she could not think why, that he was not Hungarian.

He certainly spoke very fluently, but there was something about him that did not quite match up to the many Hungarians she had met when her father was in Vienna.

"I saw you come off the Express Train that has just arrived," the man went on conversationally, "and because you were so *chic* I was certain that you must have come from Paris."

Vida merely inclined her head to the compliment but did not answer and he went on.

"Perhaps I should introduce myself. I am Vladimir Demidovsky,"

It was what she might have expected. She was quite certain from the way he was behaving that he was one of the many Russian agents who were always questioning anyone they thought suspect in any of the Balkan countries.

She went on eating the food she had ordered and Vladimir Demidovsky said after a moment:

"Now I have introduced myself, will you not do the same?"

He spoke in a persuasive tone, and Vida thought he was deliberately trying to charm her in a manner which might have prevailed with most young women who were on their own.

She had, however, been suspicious of him from the moment he had spoken, and she knew once again it was her instinct working and she would have to be very much on her guard.

"I am afraid, Monsieur," she said, "and you must excuse my speaking French for I have just come from Paris, that I am feeling exhausted after the long train journey and therefore not very good company."

It was an excuse he could not ignore, and she knew he was disconcerted by the way he sat back in his chair in an almost exasperated manner.

Then he snapped his fingers and when a waiter hurried to his side he ordered himself a small bottle of wine.

"Perhaps it would help you to feel better," he said, "if I offered you one of the grape brandies which are a speciality of this neighbourhood and which I am sure you will find delicious."

"Thank you very much, it is very kind of you," Vida replied, still speaking French, "but I have all the wine I need and any more would give me a headache."

Vladimir Demidovsky was obviously slightly annoyed by her attitude and she felt with a sense of amusement that perhaps it was the first time in his life he had been set down by a pretty woman.

They sat in silence for a little while and then he said:

"If you are a stranger to Hungary I am sure I could help you by recommending what you should see and whom to meet in whichever part of the country you are going."

"That is kind of you," Vida replied, "but I shall be with friends who will of course look after me most adequately."

She called the waiter as she spoke, paid for her luncheon, leaving a generous tip, and rose to leave the table.

As she did so Vladimir Demidovsky rose too.

"Please, Madame, do not leave me desolate, without knowing where you are going and distressed at the thought of not seeing you again."

"You are very flattering, Monsieur," Vida replied, "but I am sure there are many beautiful women in Budapest who would be only too willing to console you."

She smiled as if to take the sting out of her words and then walked away, aware as she did so that he was staring after her.

She was certain that he felt frustrated and annoyed that he had learnt nothing from his attempted interrogation.

Henri and Margit, having eaten in the other part of the restaurant, were waiting and they joined her as Vida walked out onto the platform.

"Who was that man talking to you?" Margit asked when they were out of earshot from anyone in the restaurant.

"A Russian agent," Vida replied, and saw the shock in the maid's eyes and in Henri's.

"How can you be sure of that?" he asked.

"He was very inquisitive in a flirtatious sort of manner, but of course I told him nothing. At the same time I have the uncomfortable feeling that he is suspicious."

"Why should he be that?" Margit asked in a hostile tone.

"Are Russian agents anything else? It has made me sure of one thing."

"What is that?"

"It would be a mistake when we get to Sarospatak to stay, as I had intended, in a hotel."

"I warned you that no hotel in that part of the country would be comfortable," Henri said.

"You are right, and therefore we will take advantage of the hospitality of the Hungarians, which is of course traditional."

"You mean you will go to the Castle?"

"Exactly. You must find out who is living there now. I am certain they will know Mama's family by name, even if they are not actually acquainted with my cousins."

"I thought you were not going to say that your mother was a Rákóczi," Margit said.

"I will be vaguely related to the family, which is a very large one," Vida answered. "In fact, there are dozens if not hundreds of them scattered all over Hungary and they may as well come in useful."

She did not say any more but merely walked up and down the platform until the train that was to carry them to the eastern part of Hungary came into the station.

It was certainly not as comfortable as the Express that had brought them from Paris, but the sleeping compartments were spotlessly clean.

As always in Hungary the attendant was cheerful, smiling and willing, and after Margit had given him a large tip, he was most willing to provide anything required.

Vida was aware that the Russian who had talked to her in the restaurant watched her board the train, and she was quite certain he had been inquisitive enough to read the labels on her luggage.

She however pretended she had not seen him and was thankful that when the train finally steamed out of the station he was left behind.

The train was too old-fashioned to have a restaurant car on it and instead it stopped every two or three hours at some town where there was a restaurant on the station.

This of course slowed down their process considerably and they did not arrive at Sarospatak until the afternoon of the second day after leaving Budapest.

The town lay on the edge of the frontier and in front of the range of the Zemplen Mountains.

While on the train Vida had been remembering what her mother had told her about the Castle which was a very old one, having been built in 1207.

Because her mother had adored her own country and was often homesick, she had taught Vida from a very early age the history of Hungary.

She had learnt how Prince Arpad, riding at the head of seven mounted Hungarian tribes, had descended on the Carpathian Basin in search of a land "rich in grass and water."

She told her how all the land south of the Danube had been conquered by the Romans, and then how after the fall of the Roman Empire the Slavs, Longobards, Avars, and the Huns had all encroached on the land and settled there.

She also taught Vida the many superstitions and

legends which all stemmed from the heathen gods. They had honoured fire, air, and water as holy and sang hymns of praise to the earth.

They also worshipped a God called Isten, and to him they sacrificed horses, oxen, and sheep, and occasionally human beings.

It was a fascinating study which Vida had continued as she grew older, because she felt it was part of her blood.

Since her father also had been deeply interested in the Balkan peoples as a whole, they had tried together to study and to understand all the separate nationalities, each with their own beliefs, their ambitions, and of course, their ever-encroaching enemies.

Vida was aware that her own ancestor, Rákŏczi, was one of the great romantic figures of Hungarian history. His Castle and estates at Sarospatak had been confiscated when he went into exile and were afterwards leased to various Nobles of the Imperial Court.

It was not difficult to find out from the attendant on the train who owned the Castle now.

It belonged now to the ancient family of Bărtik, and Vida felt sure that they would know the other great families of Hungary who clung together united in disliking both the Austrians and the Russians.

It was a custom in Hungary, which had been passed down from the earliest times, that any traveller could ask for hospitality, and it was considered unlucky to refuse his plea however inconvenient it might be.

When they had left the train and were travelling in a hired carriage they saw the Castle in front of them and Vida realised it was large enough to house a regiment of soldiers.

Very old, it looked very Hungarian and had a charm which was hard to define in words.

The servants who came to the door were elderly but dressed in an impressive livery.

When Vida asked if she could see Count Bărtik she was led through long passages, and she could see through the heavily-paned windows ornamental gardens stretching down to the narrow, brown Bogrog River which flowed so slowly she was told it was almost like a lake.

The Count and Countess Bărtik greeted her very pleasantly, and when she explained she was begging them to take pity on her and offer her the hospitality of their roof for the night they agreed without even seeming surprised at the request.

"I have heard about you," Vida said in her soft voice, "from my relatives, the Rákŏczis."

The Countess gave a cry of delight.

"You are a relative of the Rákŏczis? That is delightful! They are very old friends of my husband's and mine but alas as we live so far apart we very seldom see them these days. I suspect also the younger members of the family find us rather old and dull!"

"I am not a very near relation," Vida said quickly in case they should expect her to know more about them than she did, "but I am very proud of my Hungarian blood."

"Of course you are, my dear," the Countess said as if it would be impossible for anyone to feel anything different.

Vida was given a delightful bedroom overlooking the garden and Margit said when they were alone:

"You'll be very comfortable here, and if you're

wise you'll stay as long as you can!"

Vida shook her head.

"You know I have to go into Russia and we are not on a pleasure trip, Margit!"

The old maid sighed although she did not argue. She simply dressed Vida in one of her pretty but not spectacular gowns to dine with the Count and Countess.

When Vida went downstairs for dinner she wished she could follow Margit's advice and stay for some time to see the eastern part of Hungary she had always longed to visit.

But she knew that she was being urged by an instinct she could not deny to go to find her father as soon as possible.

She knew in a way that she could not explain that time was getting short, the sands were running out, and she must find him quickly.

'It is,' she thought desperately, 'like looking for a needle in a haystack, as Russia is such a huge country.'

Yet the Marquess had helped her by telling her that Prince Ivan might be able to show the way, but at the same time he might in fact hinder or even prevent her from reaching her father.

"I shall have to be very clever about this," she told herself.

When after a quiet, friendly evening with the Count and Countess she went to bed, she prayed with a fervency that had something desperate about it that she would not fail in her quest.

She had made herself so charming to her hosts that the next morning they begged her to stay longer and not travel into Russia immediately.

She thanked them but said it was imperative for

her to reach her destination as quickly as possible.

She had been clever enough the night before to gain a little information about Prince Ivan Pavolivski.

"I find him a charming young man," the Countess had said, "but my husband disapproves of all Russians and will not make an exception for the Prince."

"He is too rich and too powerful for my liking!" the Count said.

"In what way is he powerful?" Vida asked.

"He owns an enormous amount of land, is considered to be fabulously rich, and . . ."

The Count paused.

"Do go on!"

"I was just going to say that it often seems to me strange that he is of such account in Russia itself."

"What do you mean by that?" Vida enquired.

"It is difficult to put it into words," the Count replied. "Pavolivski is from an old family but there is nothing particularly unusual about their history. Yet the Prince seems to have an influence out of proportion to his breeding and his title, both in St. Petersburg and here."

The Countess laughed.

"I am afraid my husband is suspicious of everything Russian. The Prince keeps up his estates well and is, I am told, kind to his serfs, which is more than most Russians are."

"I thought the serfs were set free by Alexander II," Vida said.

"Yes, ostensibly they were," the Countess replied, "but they have to work to live, earn money to eat, and sadly some landowners still treat their people disgracefully."

"A lot of things are disgraceful in Russia!" the

Count said heavily. "First and foremost the Tzar himself!"

The Countess looked nervously over her shoulder.

"Be careful, my dear," she said. "These days even the walls have ears and you know as well as I do the Secret Police are everywhere."

"We should be safe in our own country!" the Count growled.

"So we should," his wife agreed. "At the same time, strange things happen to many of our people, and we do live on the border."

As she was obviously frightened at the way her husband was speaking, Vida did not press him to say any more.

But as she drove away early the next morning, she was thinking that it was very wrong that people should be afraid of their neighbours in their own houses and in their own country.

Russia was undoubtedly a menace to Hungary, as it was to India.

She had instructed Henri as soon as they had arrived at the Castle to purchase for her the very best horses available and a carriage which would carry her over the border to the Prince's Castle which was actually only twenty-five miles away.

Henri had been sensible enough to consult the Count's Head Groom and with his help managed to purchase a superb pair of horses which were exactly what Vida had wanted to own.

The carriage was slightly old-fashioned, but at the same time well-sprung, and the hood could be opened or shut according to the weather.

It had cost her a considerable sum of money, but

Vida could afford it and she had no intention of skimping and saving on anything that concerned her father.

It was however not easy to move swiftly once they had set out towards the mountains.

The roadway of the pass through them was rough and rocky and it was only when they were actually in Russia and had reached comparatively level ground they were able to make progress.

It was therefore, rather to Vida's consternation, getting late in the afternoon when finally she saw in front of them, surrounded by a forest and with a great lake in front of it, the Pavolivski Castle.

It was very much more ornate and appeared to be much more recently built or renovated than the one she had just left.

There were towers and domes glinting in the afternoon sun, and what seemed to her a thousand windows gleaming like diamonds across a wide expanse of green.

It actually had a fairy-tale appearance and seemed almost unreal.

However it was so beautiful that she felt her spirits rise, and her apprehension about her father, which had become more and more acute in the last twenty-four hours, seemed to lift a little.

"I am sure the Prince will help me," she told herself reassuringly, although she could not really be certain of anything.

The horses had been obviously tiring, though they had driven them slowly and had had several rests during the journey when they had stopped for food.

But now as they drew nearer to the Castle they quickened their pace, as if they knew good stabling was waiting for them.

They swept under high arches and through a huge gateway which led into a courtyard.

Then there was a magnificent flight of stone steps leading up to an impressive front door with pillars, urns, and beautifully carved statues which as well as being very attractive were rather awe-inspiring.

Henri got out to ask if His Highness the Prince would receive the Countess Vida Kărólzi and there was a long pause before the servant, resplendent in claret livery ornamented with a great deal of gold braid, returned to say:

"His Highness will receive the Countess."

At the last stop Vida had spent a great deal of time over her appearance.

She had darkened further her already dark, long eye-lashes, used a lip-salve on her lips, and powdered her small, straight nose.

Wearing a hat trimmed with feathers she looked, she knew, slightly theatrical. At the same time she would have been mock-modest if she did not realise that she looked exceedingly attractive.

Her hair was not the flaming red that was so often associated with Hungarian women, but the dark auburn that the Viennese claimed as their own, but was really of Hungarian origin.

With it, her skin was not only very white but translucent, like a pearl, and had a quality which was seldom seen in women of any nationality.

"We must be very careful what we do," she had said to Margit and Henri just before they arrived.

She knew it was something she also must remember as she walked slowly and with dignity up the steps to the front door.

The servant bowed to her and went ahead to lead her into what she saw at once was a superlatively furnished Castle, containing treasures she had never expected to find, even in Russia.

A quick glance at the pictures told her that they were all Old Masters, but what impressed her most were the sculptured marble fireplaces, painted ceilings, tapestries on the walls, and where there were no tapestries, brocade set into wood of every description.

They walked a long way over Persian carpets before the flunkey in front of her threw open a large door.

Walking through it Vida saw she was in a room with diamond-paned windows reaching almost to the lofty ceiling, and at the far end of it against a fireplace which she knew must be a unique work of art, was standing the Prince.

Everything she had heard about him had prepared her to find him very impressive, but when she saw him she realised he was not only younger than she had imagined but also far more handsome.

His dark hair swept back from a square forehead. His distinguished aristocratic features might have seemed normal in any nobleman, but his expression was different from that of any man she had met before.

His dark eyes penetrated through her as she glanced towards him.

He was dressed in a fastidious style and he might have been a Dandy from a previous era. At the same time he was overwhelmingly masculine and Vida knew instinctively his physique was powerful.

As she reached him she realised he was looking at

her with a faint expression of surprise.

"I hope, Your Highness, you will forgive me for imposing upon you," Vida said in French, "but I am invoking the old tradition of hospitality which exists in Hungary, and I hope in Russia, in asking if I may beg from you a roof over my head for tonight."

"My Castle is of course at your disposal," the Prince replied, "but I am intrigued to know why you are here and where you can be going."

"That is more simple than it appears," Vida replied. "I am on my way to Odessa. I stayed last night at the Castle Sarospatak."

She gave him a little smile before she added:

"Unfortunately I was somewhat late in rising and since the road through the mountains was far more difficult than I expected I cannot now reach the town where I had intended to stay the night, for it will be too dark to see the way."

"I understand perfectly," the Prince said. "The road through the mountains is always unpredictable and falls of rock frequently make it impassable."

"Then you will understand that my horses are tired, and so am I."

"Then that is certainly something we must remedy, Countess," he said.

He rang a small gold bell that stood on one of the tables and instantly the door opened and a servant stood there.

The Prince, speaking rapidly in his own language, gave instructions that the Countess's horses were to be stabled and her luggage taken to a bedroom. He also ordered a bottle of champagne.

While he was speaking Vida walked across the

room to the window and looked out.

She was not surprised to see a garden exquisitely laid out in the formal fashion often to be seen in Chateaux in France.

There was a huge stone fountain throwing its water iridescent towards the sky, and a number of marble statues.

When the Prince had finished giving his orders he went over to her.

"Your Castle might have stepped straight from a fairy-story," she said.

"That is obviously where you belong," he replied.

She gave a little smile but did not look at him, and after a moment he said:

"Come to sit down. I want to hear why you are travelling alone in Russia, which seems to me a remarkably foolhardy thing to do."

"I can look after myself," Vida said lightly, "and actually I have no-one to travel with me since my husband . . . died."

"You are a widow?"

"Yes, but I have reverted to my own name since I think that is one of the ways to prevent oneself from feeling unhappy."

She spoke with what she hoped was a sad note in her voice and did not look at the Prince, although she was aware that his eyes were upon her face.

Then as she sat down on a comfortable sofa he sat in a chair almost opposite her and said:

"Tell me more. You cannot suddenly have materialised from Hungary as if you were Aphrodite rising from the foam."

"Actually I have come from Paris." Vida smiled.

"And you are Russian?"

Vida made a little gesture with her hands.

"Partly," she said, "but I also have some Hungarian blood in my veins."

"A very intriguing mixture," the Prince said, "and if you are what the English would call a 'mongrel,' so am I."

"Indeed?"

"Yes, my mother was half English and half French."

Vida stared at him in surprise. This was something no-one had told her before and she had assumed that he was wholly Russian.

'This could be the reason,' she thought, 'why apart from a love of gambling he goes to Monte Carlo every year and why he visited England.'

"Which country do you find most compatible?" she asked.

"That is a very difficult question," the Prince replied, "and I suppose it is symbolic that while my name is Russian and my home is Russian, I am situated on the border."

It was a clever evasion of what she wanted to know, and Vida laughed.

"I cannot imagine you being anything but Russian."

"Why?" he asked abruptly.

"Because of all I have heard about you."

"Now you do intrigue me. What have you heard?"

Vida smiled.

"That you are very powerful; that you are feared by a great number of people; and that you are held in adulation by the whole of my sex."

This was daring, but the Prince laughed.

"I am flattered, Countess," he said, "that you should be interested to learn so much about me. I only wonder how true your information is."

"I hope it is," Vida said, "since that makes it so much more . . . interesting to know you."

She paused before the word *interesting* because she had been about to say *exciting,* but thought this might have been too forward.

There was a twinkle in the Prince's eyes, which told her he had read her thoughts and knew what she had been about to say.

Servants came in with champagne and after she had drunk a little and had eaten a few spoonfuls of the caviar that had accompanied it, Vida said:

"If I am fortunate enough to be invited to dine with Your Highness, I think that perhaps I should start to change from my dusty travelling clothes."

"They do not look in the least dusty to me," the Prince replied, "but perhaps you would like a rest. There is no hurry, for I am afraid I keep late hours and would not wish you to retire too early."

"It depends how long a journey I will have to undertake tomorrow."

"One thing is quite impossible," the Prince said, "and that is for you to leave tomorrow. First of all it would be cruel to your horses, and secondly cruel to me."

"That is certainly something I must consider," Vida replied lightly.

As the Prince handed her over to a servant who led her up a magnificently carved gold staircase to the next floor, she thought she was certainly progressing easily on the route she had set herself.

She was in the Castle, she had met the Prince, and he had already invited her to stay longer than was required by the customary hospitality that an ordinary stranger could expect.

Margit was waiting for her in her bedroom, which was as splendid as the rest of the Palace.

The bed stood in an alcove with silk curtains falling from an elaborate gold corolla which reached the ceiling. There were white bear-skin rugs on either side of the bed and everywhere one was likely to put one's feet.

The furniture was Louis XIV and the pictures on the wall by Fragonard.

It was so beautiful and at the same time so magnificent that as Vida gazed around Margit said:

"This place isn't real. If it disappeared and I woke up I wouldn't be the least surprised."

Vida laughed.

"That is what I have been feeling too."

Margit was taking the gowns out of Vida's trunk and hanging them up in the wardrobe.

"Now, what are you going to wear tonight?" she asked. "I am told there is a large party."

"A party!" Vida exclaimed.

She was surprised because as she had found the Prince alone she had somehow assumed that she would be dining with him alone and they would have a *tête-à-tête*.

"The Steward tells me there are always twenty or thirty people staying in the house with His Highness," Margit explained, "and they seldom get to bed before dawn."

"In that case," Vida said, "I must lie down and

rest. I want to have my wits about me."

"That is what I thought," Margit agreed.

She helped Vida undress and then pulled the curtains over the windows, shutting out the last rays of sunshine, and left her alone.

It was nine o'clock before Vida went downstairs for dinner, wearing one of the more elaborate, somewhat theatrical gowns she had bought especially for this visit.

She had thought since the Prince's Castle was so isolated, there would not be any competition.

Yet now she felt she had been foolish in not foreseeing that with his reputation he would expect to be amused and would make sure that there was not one hour in the day that he would be bored.

In Monte Carlo he would give parties like those the Grand Dukes gave in their Villas, with dancing, gambling, and a profusion of beautiful women. She had been naïve to think his way of life would not be the same in Russia.

She had chosen a dress which was one of the most sophisticated she had bought. As it sparkled and shimmered with every movement she made, it certainly looked most alluring.

Yet she was slightly worried in case she had chosen the wrong role for herself.

It might have been wiser to pose as an unsophisticated young girl seeking the protection of a strong man!

It was, however, too late now. She was dressed for the part that she must play and there was no looking back.

Her gown, which was green with flounces around

the hem, was a perfect foil for her dark red hair and her white skin.

Around her neck she wore a necklace of emeralds which had belonged to her mother and on her head a small tiara of the same stones.

"It certainly makes you look older than you are," Margit said as she finished dressing Vida, "and I suppose you know what you are doing. If you ask me you will find yourself in a lot of trouble if you're not careful."

The remark was so like Margit that Vida laughed.

"You are not very encouraging!"

"Well, I am not interfering," Margit said, "but just you watch your step where that Prince is concerned. I have heard things about him before now, and Henri tells me they talk about his 'harem' as if it were something clever."

Vida drew in her breath, then told herself that the fact that the Prince was susceptible to women made her task easier. Nothing mattered except, if he knew where her father was, to get him to help her.

At the same time, as she walked behind the servant who was waiting to escort her to the Salon where they were to meet before dinner, her heart was beating frantically and she was conscious that a hundred butterflies were fluttering inside her breast.

Then she raised her head a little higher.

"Why should I be frightened of anyone?" she asked herself. "If he cannot tell me what I want to know, the sooner I leave the better!"

The terrifying thing in that case was that she had no idea whatever where she should go next, and as the servant reached the Salon door she was sending out her thoughts towards her father.

"Help me, Papa! Help me!" she was saying in her heart. "I cannot manage all this without you. You must help me!"

chapter three

THE party was certainly one of wild gaiety.

To begin with Vida had been overcome by the beauty and elegance of the Prince's guests.

When she had gone downstairs and was escorted from the hall by one of the footmen, she had heard the laughter and chatter of voices coming from the Salon even before the door was opened.

Everybody was, as she expected, speaking French, and it was impossible to imagine any of the ladies present could have been dressed anywhere but in Paris.

Her father had often told her how the Russian Court favoured France not only in speaking that country's language, but also in having French tutors for their children.

What was more, the nobles all gravitated towards Paris as if it were a special Paradise created for them.

It was obvious at a quick glance that Worth had dressed the beautiful women clustered around the Prince, and Vida was immediately glad that her gown, which had seemed theatrical in London, did not look dowdy in this highly competitive scene.

As she moved down the Salon under the huge crystal chandeliers, the Prince moved towards her and she thought that he looked even more magnificent and overwhelming in his evening-clothes than he had done in the daytime.

He kissed her hand and she fancied his eyes flickered over the emeralds she wore in her hair and then at those round her neck before he said:

"My guests are all eager to meet you, Countess, and there is no need for me to tell you how beautiful you look."

He offered her the compliment in the manner she might have expected, and in French it had a smoothness which made her feel it was more polite than personal.

She, however, gave him a somewhat provocative little smile and looked up at him from under her carefully mascaraed eye-lashes.

When she met his eyes she felt uncomfortably that he was being perceptive about her and she was afraid he would penetrate her disguise.

She was therefore glad to greet his guests and receive the compliments of the gentlemen and the somewhat searching glances from the ladies.

The Prince explained how she had found the pass through the mountains very restricting and her journey had taken much longer than she had intended.

Amid exclamations of sympathy Vida had the uncomfortable feeling that the Prince was well aware she had intended to stay in his Castle and there was nothing accidental about it.

Then she told herself she was being needlessly apprehensive and there was no reason why he should suspect she was anything but what she purported to be.

Because she was a newcomer the Prince announced that he was taking her into dinner.

They proceeded into the huge and very beautifully decorated Dining-Room, where she found she was sitting on his right, even though there were a number of ladies in the party of very much higher rank.

Nobody asked her any awkward questions until the gentleman on her other side said:

"I cannot remember ever meeting anybody with the name of Kǎrólzi before. Where is your family seat situated?"

Vida had anticipated this question would be asked sooner or later and she replied:

"I am afraid there are very few of my family left now. We lived when we were in Russia, although I have never been there, in the Caucasus, near the border with Georgia. My father used to tell me it was very beautiful, but alas, I have never seen where my ancestors once were considered powerful."

"A sad story," the gentleman replied, "and something that might apply to quite a number of Russians. Your father preferred Western Europe?"

"He liked travelling," Vida answered, "and when he was not travelling you will not be surprised to hear that he enjoyed living in Paris."

"A place I also enjoy, and where the majority of

my friends find everything a man could possibly desire."

Vida looked at the faces of the ladies round the table and thought she had never seen a more beautiful assembly anywhere else in the world.

As if he knew what she was thinking the Prince on the other side of her said:

"As you see, I am a connoisseur of beautiful people as well as of antiques."

"That is your reputation, and you certainly live up to it," Vida replied. "If you really are kind enough to allow me to stay tomorrow, I hope I may see some of your treasures."

"I am looking forward to showing them to you," the Prince replied, "but I thought it might amuse you if we had a luncheon picnic in the loveliest place on my estate, which I also like to think is one of the most beautiful in all Russia."

"I find it very hard to refuse such a suggestion."

"I would not allow you to do so," he said quietly.

Vida knew in a strange way that he was trying to dominate her and told herself she must be very, very careful.

The food at dinner was as good as any she had eaten in Paris, and the wine complemented it.

When they all moved together, French fashion, from the Dining-Room she found they were in a different Salon from the one where they had assembled before dinner.

There was a polished floor in the centre of the room, which was obviously meant for dancing, and a string orchestra was playing soft and romantic music which made Vida long to waltz.

Without even asking her the Prince put his arm

around her and drew her onto the floor.

Then as they began to dance the tune that had been soft and seductive became a call from the heart which she found impossible to resist.

It was like being surrounded by flowers and feeling their fragrance becoming part of her imagination until she thought of herself as living in one of her own fairy-stories.

She was the Princess partnered by Prince Charming in a land of happiness where nothing unpleasant ever happened.

As if the Prince felt the same, although she knew of course it could not be so, he pulled her a little closer to him and they danced in silence as if speech would have interrupted the magic of their imaginations.

Then as the dance came to an end the Prince drew her from the room where they had been dancing into a Conservatory which opened out of it.

She saw it was filled with exotic flowers, all lit in the amazing way which her father had described to her as peculiar to the Winter Palace in St. Petersburg.

There were lights that shone behind the leaves of the orchids and the lilies, making them transparent; there were lights which illumined flowers growing on the floor and flowers hanging from the ceiling.

Everything seemed to be in bloom and it was an enchantment which made Vida feel once again it could only be part of a fairy-story.

Looking up at the flowers above her she clasped her hands together and said:

"It is so lovely that I know it can only be part of a dream."

"As you are!" the Prince said very quietly. "I am

only afraid you will vanish in the same unaccountable manner in which you arrived."

"I will not do that until I have seen everything in this magical Castle," Vida said.

"Thank you," he answered, "and now come and hear some music which comes from our neighbours and which I feel you will appreciate."

The string orchestra had now been replaced by a band of Hungarian Gypsies.

They were very colourful, the women wearing full red skirts with velvet bodices, and the men with their sashes glistening with jewelled weapons.

Vida had always heard that the Russians appreciated Gypsy music, and were in fact kinder to the Gypsies than were any other nation in Europe.

She realised at once that these performers were particularly talented, not only in their playing but also in their dancing when she knew she was watching women who could rival any ballerina, however acclaimed.

Now the tempo of the party seemed to rise with the Gypsy melodies.

The dancing became wilder and it seemed to Vida that her heart beat quicker and she became irrepressibly excited.

Although she danced with two or three other gentlemen, the Prince seemed to claim her for dance after dance.

She deliberately ignored what she thought were angry and questioning glances from one of the ladies in particular, who looked even more beautiful than the others.

Only when once again the Prince had taken Vida into the Conservatory to look at the lights on the flowers did the lady come in behind them to exclaim:

"Do you intend to neglect me, Ivan, for the whole evening? I cannot imagine why you should be so cruel to me when I have come such a long way to visit you."

"I am sorry, Eudoxia, if I have seemed neglectful," the Prince replied lightly, "but I cannot allow a new-comer who knows nobody else in the party to feel she is not being properly entertained."

Princess Eudoxia gave a spiteful look at Vida who said quickly to the Prince:

"As it happens, Your Highness, I was just about to ask you to excuse me if I retire to bed. It has been for me a long and very exhausting day, and I am finding it difficult to keep my eyes open."

"Then I must not try to persuade you to stay up," the Prince said, "and there is always tomorrow."

"Of course," Vida agreed, "and I am looking forward to your picnic."

He escorted her to the bottom of the stairs, then lifting her hand he held it in both of his before he said:

"You promise you will not disappear during the night back to Olympus, or wherever it is you came from, so that I shall not see you in the morning?"

"I promise."

She laughed as she spoke, then as she looked into the Prince's eyes she found the sound dying away on her lips.

For a moment they just looked at each other, then he bent his handsome head and kissed her hand.

It was not a perfunctory gesture, and she could feel his lips hard and sensuous on her skin.

Then suddenly afraid of the feelings it evoked within

her, she took her hand from his and ran up the staircase without looking back.

Margit was waiting for her in her bedroom.

"You should not have stayed up!" Vida exclaimed. "You must be very tired."

"I am seeing you properly into bed, Miss Vida," Margit said in English, "and making sure you lock your door."

"Be careful!" Vida said in a low voice. "And do remember to call me M'Lady."

"There's nobody here who speaks English," Margit said. "You may be sure of that!"

"We cannot be sure of anything!"

Vida knew as she spoke she was not in the least sure about the Prince. In fact she was afraid of him.

It was something she felt again the next day when, having awoken late because Margit said no-one was being called early, she found him waiting for her.

Outside the front door there was an array of carriages of every sort and description, all drawn by the most superbly outstanding horses Vida had ever seen.

She could not help admiring first one, then another, perceiving that the majority of them had been bred in Hungary and were therefore, as she had always known, superior to any other horses in Europe.

The Prince accompanied her, a faint smile on his lips, as if he were amused by her enthusiasm.

"Now that you have admired these," he said, "you must see the many horses in my stables which are too good to be driven, but which I know you would appreciate if you were in the saddle."

"I may not be here tomorrow."

"That is something we will argue about later," the Prince said.

The rest of the party appeared and they all seemed to be paired off, so that inevitably Vida found herself in a chaise with the Prince.

There was no sign of Princess Eudoxia and Vida wondered if she was staying behind because she was sulking, or whether she had left the Castle.

She was however too tactful to ask questions, and they drove off, the women looking, she thought, in the sunshine like a collection of exotic birds in their feathered or flowered bonnets and wearing Parisian gowns.

They all held small sunshades to protect their skin from the bright sun.

They drove for nearly an hour on a driveway which had been cut through the thick fir woods, then came unexpectedly on a small lake surrounded entirely by trees, except where at one end of it there was a silver cascade pouring down from the mountains which towered above them.

It was, Vida saw, so lovely that it seemed like a mystical painting that could not actually be real.

The contrast between the dark green trees, the mountaintops above, on which there were still traces of snow, and the cascade pouring down into the bottomless lake was spectacular.

The banks round the lake had been planted with a profusion of iris—gold, purple, and white—that were all in bloom and they were as exquisite as the orchids she had seen last night in the Prince's Conservatory.

There was a large wooden hut to be seen amongst the trees built of logs.

They stopped at the very edge of the lake, where a table had been laid for their picnic.

The luncheon was, in fact, the height of luxury with

servants in livery to wait on them and dishes that were as delicious as at dinner the night before.

They drank French champagne from golden goblets, and after the main courses the table was piled with the local fruits: strawberries, peaches, raspberries, nectarines, melons, and in strange contrast passion fruit and pomegranates.

"The whole trouble is," Vida smiled, "it is impossible to eat any more."

"I see you enjoy your food," the Prince said, "and that pleases me."

"Why?"

"It tells me that you are still very young, and not worrying as so many women do, about your figure," he answered.

She felt guiltily that she had perhaps betrayed herself and revealed the fact that she was younger than she was pretending to be.

Then she hoped he was just paying her a compliment and it would be a mistake to be worried about it.

"I find the Russian air makes me hungry," she said.

"I think too it has done you good," the Prince answered. "You do not look as worried as you did last night when you arrived."

"Worried?" Vida questioned. "As I told you, I was tired."

"And worried," he persisted, "or perhaps nervous."

She turned away from him a little petulantly.

"I cannot think why you should imagine such things," she said. "If I was worried, it was only because I was afraid you might be inhospitable enough to say that your Castle was full and I should have to sleep the night in one of your barns!"

The Prince laughed. But she told herself that she must be more careful and that he was far too perceptive.

The luncheon had been very enjoyable, with everybody laughing and talking in an animated way across the table, which Vida thought made the meal much more fun than if it was formal.

As they finished the Prince said to her:

"Would you like to see behind the cascade?"

"Could I do that?"

"Come with me," he replied.

They walked slowly round the small lake until they came to the cascade, where it was difficult to hear oneself speak because of the roar of the water.

Then the Prince took Vida's hand and drew her through what appeared to be a gap in the rock.

For a minute or so they were in darkness and she could only let him guide her, conscious as he did so of the strength of his fingers.

She had the feeling that as he touched her there was something magnetic about it that she had never known with anybody else.

The dark passage came to an end and she found herself standing in a huge cave, the blinding silver curtain of water in front of her as it crashed down from the mountain heights into the lake below.

It was so lovely, a shimmering wall of silver, and the noise of it seemed somehow to deaden the senses so that Vida felt she could no longer think but only feel somehow disembodied and part of the beauty and sound of the water itself.

Then she was aware that while she was looking at

the cascade, the Prince was looking at her.

There was something in his eyes that made her feel nervous, and without speaking she moved back towards the passage.

Only as she reached the entrance in the rock did she look back and see he had not moved but was still standing looking at her.

As she waited for him to come to her, she had a very strong feeling that he was calling her, almost hypnotising her to come to him.

For one fleeting moment she felt she had to obey.

Then with what was both a mental and a physical effort she began to walk very slowly through the dark tunnel in front of her.

She put out her hands on either side to guide her and reached the sunshine before the Prince joined her.

They walked away from the cascade and with an effort Vida managed to say lightly:

"Thank you, that was a unique experience!"

"I thought you would enjoy it," the Prince said simply.

They joined the others, then drove back to the Castle.

There was tea made in the Russian way for those who required it, and caviar sandwiches and various sweet-meats to go with it.

There was champagne for the gentlemen or any other drink they fancied.

Vida found that the ladies were expected to rest before dinner, and she therefore went with them up to her bedroom, where Margit was waiting for her.

To her surprise while Margit was undoing her gown she spoke to her almost in a whisper and appeared to be nervous.

"Say little, M'Lady, not safe!"

Vida nodded her head to show she understood.

When she was resting in bed she wondered what Margit knew, and how she could be safely alone with her to find out.

'Perhaps we could go into the garden together,' she thought. She remembered how her father had always said that it was safer to talk out of doors than anywhere else.

She slept a little, and when Margit came to call her there was no time for anything but to put on another of her specially chosen gowns.

Only when she was almost ready to go downstairs to the Dining-Room did she draw Margit across the room to the open window.

Speaking softly into her ear she asked:

"What have you found out, Margit?"

"Not much," Margit replied in English, "but enough to make me worried! Tonight I will try to talk with His Highness's valet."

"A good idea!" Vida said. "But do not wait up, as I may be late and I can undo this gown quite easily."

"You sure?"

"Quite sure!"

She was used to looking after herself, and because Margit was growing old she never allowed her to stay up late waiting for her as was customary for a lady's-maid.

"It is too much for you," she had said when Margit had expostulated, "and there is so much to do in the daytime that I do not want you to feel you cannot cope."

She said again now:

"Go to bed, and I will find some way to talk to you in the morning."

Margit nodded to show she understood. Then she said quickly:

"You lock the door?"

"Of course!" Vida agreed.

She felt quite certain the Prince would not approach her.

At the same time it was always wise to take precautions, and she remembered how her mother had often told her when she was young and staying in hotels or in private houses to lock her bedroom door in case of thieves.

Once again the Prince took her into dinner and they had, Vida thought, one of the most interesting conversations she had ever enjoyed about the treasures that had been collected in Russia by Catherine the Great.

They also discussed the treasures he himself possessed in this and other of his houses.

She thought, although he had not spoken of it, that he was surprised at how much she knew about art.

They talked about the Gypsies and their dancing, and she found that this was a particularly enjoyable subject.

"I am glad you enjoy dancing," the Prince said, "because tonight I have a treat for you."

"What is it?"

"I have arranged for a ballet to be performed in my private theatre, and since the ballerinas come from Moscow I think you will find they are outstanding."

"That is the most exciting thing I have ever heard!" Vida exclaimed enthusiastically.

The Prince's private theatre was small but beautiful, with very comfortable upholstered chairs in which to sit.

The curtains which draped the proscenium were of the richest and most exquisite brocade and everywhere there were gilded carvings that Vida could see had been executed by exceptional craftsmen.

As soon as they were all seated the orchestra struck up the overture, and when the curtains were drawn back Vida knew the Prince had been correct in saying that the ballerinas were exceptional.

She found it difficult to remember when she had last seen such exquisite dancing, even though she had often attended ballet performances in Vienna as well as in Paris.

She forgot the Prince, she forgot everything except the story being unfolded in mime and the beauty of the music to which the professionals danced.

Only as the curtain fell was she aware that the Prince's eyes were on her face and not on the stage.

She gave a deep sigh as if she came back to earth from another planet and said:

"That was wonderful!"

"I think you felt as if you were dancing with them yourself," the Prince said.

"Of course I did! And I was part of the story they were telling!"

"I knew that," he replied. "Your eyes are very expressive and very revealing."

"I hope not," Vida said quickly.

"Why not?" he enquired.

"It is said that the eyes are the mirror of the soul," she answered, "and I have no wish to have anybody looking into my soul or any other part of me that is strictly private."

"I think that is something you cannot altogether prevent," he answered. "And may I say that I find your soul as entrancing as I find everything else about you?"

There seemed to be a different note in his voice from the way he had spoken before, but Vida told herself quickly that he was just being politely complimentary, as any other young man might be.

And yet she was not sure.

She knew that the Russian character was very different from that of any other nationality.

Unlike an Englishman, a Russian's soul was so consciously a part of himself that he thought of it and spoke of it as something quite familiar and very precious.

He was not at all embarrassed by it, and where an Englishman felt with his heart, a Russian felt with his soul, and his emotions therefore came from the very depths of his being.

When they left the theatre there were refreshments in yet another room in which they could dance.

Tonight, as if the haunting beauty of the ballet still lingered with them, there was a string orchestra to play the Offenbach waltzes which had captured the hearts of all Paris.

To Vida's surprise, the orchestra stopped playing far earlier than she expected, and the Prince made it obvious without actually saying so that he was waiting for his guests to retire to bed.

"You must be planning something very interesting for us tomorrow, Your Highness," one of the gentlemen said. "How early are we starting?"

"Earlier than usual," the Prince replied, "but you will be called in plenty of time to dress without hurry, and enjoy your breakfast."

"You are making me curious," his guest remarked.

"That is what I want you to be," the Prince smiled.

He escorted Vida to the bottom of the stairs, but tonight as she was not going up alone, he bowed over her hand instead of kissing it.

She went up the stairs talking to several of the ladies who seemed extremely friendly.

They admired Vida's gown which tonight had been white and silver, and made her look like a nymph rising from below the cascade they had seen at luncheontime.

Instead of the jewels which had made her look so resplendent last night she wore a wreath of camelias in her hair, and the same flowers decorated her gown.

Round her neck she wore her mother's five rows of pearls, and there were pearls in her ears and on her wedding-finger.

The Prince had not commented upon her appearance, but she had known by the expression in his eyes that he thought she looked beautiful.

When she went into her bedroom and locked her door, as she had promised Margit she would do, she told herself she had never had a more enjoyable time.

She had however got no further in discovering what had happened to her father since she had entered Russia.

"What am I to do?" she asked herself.

Then she decided that tomorrow she must play about no longer. She must make up her mind whether or not she could trust the Prince and ask his help.

"He must be trustworthy," she tried to assure herself.

And yet she was afraid.

She knew that all through the day, even at the cascade, underlying her appreciation of everything that had been planned was an ache within her, almost a physical pain, which told her her father was in danger.

'I cannot go on like this!' she thought as she lifted the wreath from off her head and put away her gown in the wardrobe.

When she was in bed she found herself sending out her thoughts to her father, begging him to guide and help her.

"Can I trust the Prince, Papa?" she asked.

"Dare I tell him the truth as to why I am here?"

Because she felt so agitated she lit two candles by her bed and picked up the small Bible with which she always travelled.

Her mother had given it to her on her tenth birthday and said:

"If you are ever worried, my darling, if you want the answer to any problem, however complex, look in your Bible."

"Do you mean open it at random, Mama?" Vida had asked.

"What I do," her mother replied, "is to pray, then open it with my eyes shut and put my finger on one verse, and very seldom do I not get an answer."

"That is what I will do now," Vida decided.

She held the Bible in her hand, shut her eyes, and as she did so she heard a sound.

She looked up and saw to her astonishment that at the far end of the room a panel in the wall had opened and the Prince came in.

For a moment she could only stare at him, wondering if she had shut the door and locked it.

He came towards her, a smile on his lips, and she saw that he was wearing a long velvet robe which reached almost to the floor and made him seem larger and in a way more menacing than he did when he was dressed.

Vida put the Bible down beside her. Then she asked:

"What . . . do you . . . want?"

"I should have thought that was obvious," the Prince replied with a faint smile. "I want to be alone with you, Vida, and I think you are aware of how much I want you."

"You cannot mean . . . ?" Vida began.

Then as if she suddenly understood, she said:

"No, no! Of course not! You must go . . . away at once!"

The Prince sat down on the bed facing her.

"Why should I do that?" he asked. "You are so beautiful and I cannot believe that you intend to go on mourning your dead husband for very much longer."

Because of the depth of his voice when he spoke and because he looked so overwhelmingly handsome in the candlelight, Vida for a moment found it impossible to answer him.

She could only look at him and her eyes seemed to fill her whole face.

She had no idea that with her dark red hair falling over her shoulders, her skin very white in contrast, and her nightgown so diaphanous that it was almost transparent, she looked like something out of a dream.

"You have captivated me since the first moment I saw you," the Prince was saying. "I find everything about you irresistible, and I believe, unless I am much mistaken, that I attract you a little."

Once again Vida felt as if he were hypnotising her and drawing her towards him so that although he had not moved she was already in his arms and he was holding her.

The thought was frightening and she put up her hands as if to safe-guard herself, saying:

"Please . . . do not talk to me like this . . . not here! Let us wait until . . . tomorrow."

"Why tomorrow?" the Prince asked. "Why not now?"

As he spoke he put out his arms and almost before Vida could realise what was happening, his lips were on hers.

For a second she could not believe that he was really kissing her, then as she felt his lips hard, insistent, and demanding on hers, she knew she had to fight against him.

But because he had pushed her back onto the pillows and was bending over her, it was impossible.

Now she tried to force him away, but his lips became more demanding, more passionate.

She felt as if he captured and possessed her so that she had no will and no thoughts of her own.

Instead, she could only feel sensations that she had no idea existed rising within her and making her feel as if he carried her up into the sky and made her part of the stars so that she was no longer herself.

Then suddenly she remembered her father, and

forcing her head to one side she managed to say:

"Please, please, you must . . . not do this to me. I cannot let you!"

"Do you really think you can stop me?" the Prince asked. "You want me, my beautiful, as I want you!"

"That is . . . not true," Vida tried to say.

He turned her face back to his, and once again his lips possessed hers and he was kissing her now with a passion that seemed to sear its way through her like a raging fire.

She was aware too that he was lying on top of the bed and she was afraid as she had never been afraid before.

"Please, please . . ." she begged.

Then as he moved his lips from her mouth to the softness of her neck she said:

"Listen to me, please, listen to me. You are . . . frightening me . . . and there is nobody to . . . help me."

"Why should you be frightened?" the Prince asked.

His lips were still against her neck, and yet for the moment he was not kissing her.

"There is . . . something I . . . came here to . . . ask you," Vida said, "but I did not . . . know you would behave . . . like this . . . and I am not certain if I can trust . . . you."

Because she was so frightened she spoke somewhat incoherently, and yet she was aware the Prince was listening.

"I want you desperately," he said. "Let me love you first, then we will talk afterwards."

"No, no!" Vida insisted. "I know it is . . . wrong for you to . . . love me like that and I did not . . . expect you to do so."

"Why not?" he enquired. "You have already made me aware that you have heard of my reputation, and you cannot be so foolish as to not have known you would attract me."

She did not answer and after a moment he said:

"That is what you wanted to do, is it not? That is why you came here."

She drew in her breath. Then she said:

"Yes, that is true, but I ... locked my door."

He smiled as if he could not help it.

"Being a Russian," he said, "you must be aware that in Russia there are always secret doors and hollow walls."

"I ... I did not ... think of ... that," Vida replied. "Please, be kind to me because I am so foolish that I did not ... realise the danger of what I was ... doing."

The Prince raised himself slowly.

Now in a different tone of voice he asked:

"What are you saying to me?"

In a piteous little voice because she was really afraid Vida answered:

"I ... I came here to ask you ... something very important ... to me. But I am not sure if I ... should do so."

As he looked at her searchingly it made her think that if she made the wrong decision and he was not to be trusted, she might, in the Marquess's words, be signing her father's death-warrant.

She was so apprehensive that she was trembling as she said:

"Please, do not touch me again and ... give me time to think."

"I do not understand," the Prince said.

"Perhaps I will be able to . . . explain tomorrow," Vida replied, "but . . . not now."

"Why not now?"

She looked away from him. Then she said:

"I . . . I cannot think . . . clearly when you . . . touch me."

"When I kiss you, you mean."

"Yes, when you . . . kiss me."

"And have you asked yourself the reason why?"

She did not answer, and after a moment he said:

"I think you know that there is something between us which we cannot ignore; something irresistible; something that draws you to me as I am drawn to you. You cannot deny it!"

He bent towards her as he said:

"Let me make love to you, Vida, and after that there will be no problems, no more difficulties."

It flashed through her mind that if he made love to her and it gave her the same sensations as his kisses, it would be very wonderful. She would not only touch the stars but be inside them, enveloped by their light.

Then she remembered her father and told herself that nothing mattered except that she should save his life.

"Please . . ." she said to the Prince. "Please give me a little time so that I can think clearly. What I have to decide does not concern only me."

"Everything you say makes me more puzzled and bewildered than before," the Prince answered.

"I know it sounds complicated, but I have to do things my way, so try to understand."

She was pleading with him and he was aware of how tense she was.

"You are making it very difficult for me," he said. "I thought for one moment when I kissed you and before you struggled against me that we touched the gates of Paradise together."

That was true, Vida thought wildly, but she had to forget everything except her father and the reason why she was here.

"Tell me your secret now," the Prince begged.

She knew he was being deliberately persuasive because he was genuinely curious.

"I . . . I cannot. I dare not," she murmured. "But tomorrow . . . may be . . . different."

She thought frantically that by tomorrow Margit might have found out something, or perhaps she would feel more sure then that she was doing the right thing.

She was vividly conscious of the Prince sitting beside her, and the magnetism which came from him, and all the sensations he had aroused in her.

She could still feel his lips on her neck, and she thought suddenly that almost anything was worth such ecstasy, such wonder.

Then as if she could see her father warning her she cried out:

"Go away! Go away and . . . leave me! I must . . . think! I must be . . . sure!"

She put out her hand and accidentally touched the Bible she had put down beside her.

She picked it up and said:

"When you came to me, I was praying for guidance, feeling this Bible would determine what I must do."

"You were praying?" the Prince asked in a deep voice.

76

"I felt only . . . God could . . . help me."

There was an expression on his face she did not understand. Then quite suddenly, so that she was surprised, he rose from the bed.

"Very well, Vida," he said, "I will grant you the time you have asked for to make up your mind, but I shall be thinking about you, wanting you, and asking myself if I have made a mistake."

"You are being kind and understanding," Vida said, "and it is never a mistake to be that."

The Prince smiled at her mockingly, then he said:

"Good night. I hope you gain the right answer from your Bible, for otherwise I shall be very, very disappointed."

He would have turned away, but Vida put out her hand impulsively.

"Thank you for being so understanding."

The Prince did not move.

"I am not going to touch you," he said, "for if I do, I might cease to do as you have asked and do what I myself want."

Vida put her hand protectively over her breast.

He looked at her for a long moment. Then he said:

"You have certainly closed the gates of Paradise— for tonight at any rate!"

He walked across the room, and as he reached the shadows he disappeared in the same strange way he had come, through the panelling in the wall.

Vida gave a little sigh that should have been one of relief.

At the same time, she had the feeling that she had lost something very precious, something she might never find again.

chapter four

WHEN the Prince had gone, Vida lay for some time just staring ahead of her and trying to think about what he had said to her, and what she felt.

But she found herself so bewildered by him that she was completely unable to decide what she should do.

Then suddenly she knew that the best thing would be to talk to Margit and see if she had learnt anything.

Moreover Margit, with her common sense and her down-to-earth attitude towards life, would perhaps take away the feeling of ecstasy which Vida had felt when the Prince had kissed her and she touched the stars.

She knew that Margit was in fact not far away and that by this time the Prince would have returned to his room.

She had said yesterday after their arrival:

"The Housekeeper's been very kind, and because the Castle's so big and we're strangers to it, she's put me on the same floor as you."

"That is very convenient," Vida murmured.

"I'm at the very end of this corridor," Margit said, "past His Highness's Suite, in a room that faces into the Courtyard, and it's very comfortable."

She spoke with a touch of pride which amused Vida. She knew that Margit always appreciated it when she was given privileges not accorded to other servants.

"I shall know where to find you, if I want you," Vida remarked.

"I'll be there when you want me," Margit said decisively.

Vida felt she must talk to her at once, and in Margit's room. It would be easier there because, if people could eavesdrop in her own room, it was unlikely the same applied to Margit's.

She put on a light robe over her nightgown and opened her door very quietly.

She peeped out to find, as she expected, that the corridor was not in darkness, but there were fewer lights burning than when she had come up to bed.

There was no sign of anybody about and she started to walk lightly along the thick carpet.

It was quite a way, and there were a number of rooms between hers and the Prince's Suite.

She had almost reached the lofty painted doors that she had noticed in the daytime which led into the Prince's rooms, when just ahead of her she heard a sound.

Instinctively, being afraid of being seen, she stopped and moved into the shadow of a doorway.

As she did so she saw a man appear from what she thought must be a secondary staircase which came out almost opposite the Prince's door.

The man was tall and seemed in the darkness somehow impressive.

Then without knocking he opened what Vida guessed was the outer door to the Prince's Suite and the light inside fell on his face.

As she watched him suddenly she was rigid, as if turned to stone, for the man who was just entering the Prince's Suite was Vladimir Demidovsky.

For a second she thought she must be dreaming.

Then she knew that she had been saved from betraying her father and that in no circumstances must she trust the Prince.

Vladimir Demidovsky disappeared but there was a faint streak of light from the door he had left ajar.

Knowing this was her opportunity to reach Margit without being seen, Vida hurried forward, moving on tiptoe, ready to pass the door and go on down the corridor.

Then as she reached it she heard Vladimir Demidovsky's voice speaking in Russian.

"It was hard to make him talk, Your Highness."

"But you managed it?" the Prince asked.

"I was somewhat rough with him."

"You mean you killed him?"

There were no words of reply but Vida was sure Vladimir Demidovsky nodded his head.

"He told you what you wanted to know?"

The Prince's question was sharp.

"Yes, Your Highness. Sir Harvey is in the Monastery of St. Onutri at Lvov."

It was then as Vida heard what was said that she realised she was holding her breath.

Moving with the swiftness of a frightened fawn she ran down the passage and entered Margit's room.

It was in darkness and she stood just inside the door which she shut behind her and called "Margit, Margit" in a very low voice.

"What is—it? What do you—want?" Margit asked in a sleepy tone.

Then as she knew the answer without Vida speaking she sat up in bed and lit a candle.

As she did so Vida was beside her whispering:

"Get up, Margit! We have to leave at once! I have discovered where Papa is, and we must save him!"

She had the terrified feeling that now that the Prince knew where her father was he would inform the Secret Police, and it was only a question of time before, as she had felt since the beginning of the journey, her father was either put in prison or murdered.

"Hurry, hurry!" she said.

"Now, listen, Miss Vida," Margit said slowly. "We can't leave before dawn, but I'll tell Henri, and he'll have the carriage waiting."

The calm way she spoke seemed to soothe away some of the terror that Vida was feeling.

For a moment she was no longer the clever young woman confident of organising a secret attempt to save her father's life as she had been when she left London.

She was a child who wanted somebody to look after her and protect her.

"Now, you go and get dressed, Miss Vida," Margit said slowly as if she were thinking it out. "I'll wake Henri. I know where he's sleeping. Then I'll come and pack your trunk."

"Thank you, Margit."

Vida bent forward, kissed the maid on the cheek, and said:

"Nobody could be as wonderful as you in an emergency!"

"Don't talk when we are in your bedroom," Margit said.

"I know," Vida answered, "the walls are hollow."

She did not add that there was a secret entrance, thinking if she did so Margit might guess what had happened.

Instead, she peeped out into the corridor and saw with relief that the Prince's door was closed and no longer was any light coming from it.

That meant that either Vladimir Demidovsky had shut the door, or else having given the Prince the information for which he was waiting he had then left him.

Vida ran back as swiftly as possible, and moving like a ghost along the dimly-lit corridor.

As she reached her own bedroom she was breathless.

She stood for a moment with her back to the door, trying to quell the tumult within her breast.

Then, as she realised that if nothing else she had found out where her father was, she sent out her thoughts towards him.

She was trying to tell him that she was coming to him and if it was humanly possible she would find a way to rescue him.

*　　*　　*

Later, when they were driving away from the Castle, Vida could hardly believe she had been so successful in escaping without any difficulty.

She was already dressed when Margit arrived, and started to put her things in a large trunk which fortunately was kept in a dressing-room which adjoined her room.

Margit was wearing her black travelling-clothes and looked so solid, unruffled, and dependable that Vida was ashamed of her own feelings of panic.

She did not speak and Margit merely took down the gowns from the wardrobe, folded them, and put them into the trunk.

Even as she closed the round-topped lid Henri came into the room with a young footman.

He was obviously a rather stupid boy and Vida was sure Henri had chosen him because he asked no questions, but merely did as he was told.

He and Henri carried her trunk along the corridor and avoiding the main staircase went down a secondary one which led them to a door on the ground floor which opened into a Courtyard at the back of the Castle.

Dawn was just breaking but the first rays of the sun had not appeared over the horizon.

Only the stars were fading a little in the sky and there was that hush over the world which was like a prelude to a play.

The horses that were to draw the carriage were restless, and Vida knew they were fresh after their rest of the previous day.

The coachman was on the box, Vida's trunk was strapped on behind, then as she and Margit stepped into the carriage Henri climbed up beside the coachman and they were off.

Only when she looked back and the Castle was no longer in sight did Vida feel a sense of elation, as if she had taken a high fence in a steeplechase and, although there were a great number of others ahead of her, her first effort had been faultless.

She slipped her hand into Margit's saying:

"Thank you, Margit. Nobody but you could have helped me to get away so cleverly!"

"Now, tell me exactly what you heard, Miss Vida!"

Vida told her how she had seen Vladimir Demidovsky, who had approached her in Budapest, and what she had overheard of his conversation with the Prince.

"You suspected he was a Russian Agent," Margit said.

"Yes, and we know now that the Prince is not to be trusted . . . and he too is against Papa."

There was a dull note in her voice but Margit did not notice it.

Vida was thinking that the wonder and ecstasy the Prince had aroused in her was false and only part of her imagination.

How could she feel anything like that for a man who was prepared to murder her father as Vladimir Demidovsky had murdered a man?

She was aware that the town of Lvov was a long way from the Castle, much farther than the distance they had travelled from Hungary.

The road mercifully was level and in good repair

and the horses were making excellent progress.

By the time they reached the first inn on the road, they all with the exception of Vida were hungry for something to eat.

She was so agitated that she felt it would be impossible for her ever to eat again.

The food was anyway unpalatable. At the same time the tea in its samovar was excellent and very reviving.

She could understand how the Russians, whatever else they left behind, never went anywhere without their samovars.

The horses were fed with the very best oats which Henri had been shrewd enough to instruct the coachman to purloin from the Prince's stable.

As they set out again Vida thought with joy that their pace was still good, but before long she realised she was too optimistic.

Later in the afternoon the road became much steeper, with a broken surface strewn with rocks, and thick with trees. Because of the danger of a broken axle, they were forced to go slowly.

She almost cried with vexation, but there was nothing she could do about it.

Instead, she could only pray fervently that in the monastery her father was safe, and she would reach him before the Prince and his minions were able to do so.

Then she told herself that because His Highness was so clever at being an enigma to the British Government, and perhaps even to people as astute as her father, he would not personally be involved in what happened next.

He would probably relay the information to the Tzar's Secret Police, and they would do the rest.

She felt herself shudder as she remembered the terrible crimes they had committed and the horrors they had perpetrated in Russia since Alexander III came to the throne.

His reign had opened with a persecution of the Jews that was unequalled in history.

She remembered her father telling her that over 250,000 destitute Jews had been forced out of Russia into Western Europe.

"Let them carry their poison where they will!" the Tzar had said.

There were a thousand other shameful actions which Vida could not bear to think about, but she could not suppress them and they kept recurring in her mind until she felt she would go mad.

By the time they had passed through the mountainous region it was growing dark.

There was therefore nothing they could do but spend the night in a village where the only accommodation for travellers was dirty and so inadequate that Vida felt after the comforts of the Castle they had stepped down into a bog.

She and Margit occupied a small bedroom together, and as they were quite certain the beds were verminous they slept in their clothes lying on the rugs which Henri brought in from the carriage.

Their supper consisted of a Russian soup which smelt unpleasant and tasted even worse, and thick slices of black rye bread.

There was however the inevitable but drinkable tea.

It was difficult not to think of the delicious dishes

with which she had been served the previous evening, and the caviar that had been available at any hour of the day.

But hunger, sleeplessness, and the smell of the unwashed rooms were unimportant beside the fact that she was much nearer to her father than she had been before.

At least she knew where he was, and that was all-important.

Once again they set off at dawn, and now the road was far better, although it was not possible to go as fast as Vida would have liked.

They reached their destination after a long and tiring day, hungry and feeling indescribably dusty and dirty from the journey.

The seventeenth-century monastery was just outside the town surrounded by a high wall which Henri pointed out as they passed it.

The bell tower of the church rose above it, and there was just enough light to see the heavily-barred door which Vida guessed was the only entrance.

She was already wondering despairingly how she could get in touch with her father, but it was too late that night to do anything but find somewhere to rest.

She had not only to think of herself but of Margit, who was looking very weary and, as she admitted, "feeling her age."

To their surprise there was a hotel which, while certainly not luxurious, was clean and adequate.

It had been built only in the last three years, and was used, Vida learned, mainly by commercial travellers who went from city to city selling their wares.

It was also a stopping place for those en route to the south.

At any rate there it was and the food it offered was plain but nourishing, while the beds though hard, were nothing like the verminous horrors they had endured the night before.

"Now, go to bed, Miss Vida, and sleep!" Margit said firmly. "You'll do no good worrying about the master until it's daylight. Then Henri can find out how we can contact him. Until then, remember—'a tired brain's a useless one.'"

Vida laughed as if she could not help it.

"You are marvellous, Margit!" she exclaimed. "I cannot tell you what it means to me to have you with me!"

"If I don't get some sleep," Margit retorted, "I tell you one thing, Miss Vida. I'll leave my bones in Russia, which is a place I never could abide!"

Vida laughed again. Then as Margit left her she got into bed.

Once she had blown out the candles she prayed first to her mother to help her, then she tried to send waves of thought to her father to let him know that she was near and had come to save him.

*　　*　　*

Vida must have fallen into an exhausted, dreamless sleep, for she awoke with a little start as the curtains were pulled back, and she thought Margit had come in to wake her.

Then as she opened her eyes she realised that standing against the pale light from the window was not Margit, but a man.

She caught her breath, and as he turned round she saw it was the Prince!

For a moment she was both speechless and motionless, just staring at him. She felt it could not be true that he was there, but if he was, then her journey was in vain and her father was doomed.

He saw she was awake and walked towards the bed to sit down on it, facing her.

"You look very lovely in the morning," he said in the same tone he might have used when they had been together at the Castle.

"W-why . . . are you . . . here?"

She knew the answer, and yet she had to hear him say it.

She felt that if he told her what he intended there would be nothing for her to do but die with her father.

He looked for a long moment at the terror in her eyes and the way her lips trembled with fear before he asked:

"Why did you not trust me?"

"Trust . . . you?" Vida asked. "How . . . could I do that . . . when you . . ."

She paused, wondering how she could possibly put into words what she felt sure he was about to do.

"If you had told me what you were thinking," the Prince said, "you could have saved yourself a very uncomfortable journey, and what I feel must have been an agony of apprehension."

"I . . . I do not know . . . what you mean."

She was wondering if he had found out who she was, and if in fact, he now knew that she was her father's daughter.

He might be trying to trick her, and she was therefore desperately afraid of saying the wrong thing.

"Now that you are here," the Prince said, "perhaps you will tell me how you intend to save your father."

"How did you . . . know that is . . . what I want to do?" she whispered.

"When I learnt you were Vida Anstruther," the Prince said, "everything that had been puzzling me about you fell into place."

"H-how did you . . . find out?" Vida asked weakly.

Before he could answer her she said:

"Of course! It was Vladimir Demidovsky who told you!"

"Naturally!" the Prince agreed. "I presume you must have seen him, or become aware that he was in the Castle. He told me he had spoken to you and, I thought, somewhat indiscreetly given you his name in Budapest."

"I . . . I was frightened of him. I thought he was a Russian . . . Agent!"

"He is *my* Agent," the Prince explained, "and a very effective one."

He smiled before he went on.

"He not only discovered for me where your father had hidden himself from the Tzar's men, who are pursuing him, but he also described, which I feel was very astute of him, a very lovely lady, now calling herself the Countess Vida Kărólzi, who boarded the Express Train from Paris as Miss Vida Anstruther."

"So you now know I am Papa's daughter."

"Yes, I know!"

He put out his other hand and ran his fingers along the line of her chin.

It made Vida feel as though a little flame touched her, and she quivered as the Prince said:

"How could you have been so ridiculous as to pretend to be a widow?"

"You . . . believed . . . me," she said defensively.

"Not once I had kissed you."

She felt the colour rise in her cheeks.

"What . . . did you know . . . then?"

"That you had never been kissed before," the Prince answered, "and that, my precious, was why I left you."

Vida looked at him wide-eyed.

Then as if he forced himself to do so, he released her hand and said in a different tone of voice:

"Now perhaps you will tell me how you intend to get your father away from here?"

"I . . . I do not . . . know," Vida replied. "I only know that I . . . had to . . . come to him . . . and that he is in danger."

There was a little sob in her voice as she said:

"Please, please help me!"

"That is what I intend to do," the Prince answered. "I already have a plan which I think, and hope, will work."

Vida felt a surge of excitement sweep through her at his words.

She sat up in bed and held out both her hands to him.

"Why was I so . . . foolish as not to know instinctively that . . . you would want to . . . help Papa rather than have him imprisoned or even killed, as I was . . . afraid you . . . might?"

"One day," the Prince said in a deep voice, "I will make you apologise for even suspecting that I could be a supporter of evil. But first we have to concentrate, and time is vitally important in getting your father out of the country."

Vida drew in her breath, but did not speak, simply

looked at the Prince, her eyes very wide, her dark red hair hanging over her shoulders.

"The first thing is to get him away from the monastery," the Prince said, "and I have thought of a plan for doing that."

"How can we?" Vida asked.

"You arrived here exhausted after your long journey and during the night you had a bad heart-attack," the Prince said. "You are therefore very eager to contact your Confessor, who you understand is at the moment in the Monastery of St. Onutri."

It was such a clever idea that Vida slipped her hand into the Prince's and held on to it almost as if she were afraid that before he finished explaining his plan he would disappear.

Then, despite her anxiety and her genuine weakness, she felt as if a shaft of sunlight ran through her as his fingers closed over hers so tightly that they hurt.

"I am going to send your Courier, whose name, I understand, is Henri, to see the abbot at the monastery," the Prince said. "He will say that you have come from my Castle, which will impress him, but not that I too am here."

"I am . . . sure that is . . . wise," Vida murmured.

"The fact that we do not know what name your father is using at the moment makes it more difficult," the Prince went on. "Henri can explain that you are not well enough to answer any questions. But your maid who has been with you for many years knows that the one person who can help in this emergency is your Confessor, who has known the family ever since you were a child."

"Papa does not . . . know the . . . name on . . . my

passport," Vida said quickly.

"I guessed that," the Prince said, "but Henri can say that you are the Countess *Vida* Kărólzi, and I cannot believe your father, who is very quick-witted, will not comprehend."

"You know Papa?"

"Of course I know him," the Prince answered, "and I admire him more than I can possibly say! At the same time, to enter Russia when he knew the Secret Police were waiting for him was a foolhardy action."

"I warned Papa he was a . . . marked man."

"But he would not listen to you," the Prince said, "and now I am afraid that for the rest of his life Russia is forbidden territory."

"But first we . . . have to get him . . . out."

"That is the operative word, and *we* will get him out, you and I, Vida!"

His eyes met hers and it was hard for him to look away.

Then as if he forced himself once again to concentrate on what was immediately important he said:

"I am going to find Henri now and instruct him to go to the monastery as soon as possible. The monks rise early and as soon as their first service is over he will have an opportunity to see the abbot."

"If only we knew what name Papa is using," Vida murmured.

"He will give Henri the answer to that question," the Prince said.

He rose from the bed as he spoke, smiled at her, and walked towards the door.

As he reached it he looked back and said softly:

"As I have said before, you look very lovely in the morning."

She felt herself blush. At the same time she felt as if her whole body had come alive and she was singing like a lark in the sky.

The Prince was here, he had taken over the problem from her, and was now in command.

All she wanted to do was to rest on his strength and feel the wonder of him seep through her like the sunshine.

Five minutes later Margit came hurrying to her.

"That'll teach us to make hasty opinions about anybody in the future!" she said sharply. "His Highness has just walked into my bedroom, where of course I was lying in bed, and he almost gave me a heart-attack! He's told me what has been planned, and even your father couldn't think of a cleverer idea!"

"He is wonderful!" Vida exclaimed. "I could hardly believe it when he pulled back the curtains. I thought it was you!"

"While he's giving Henri orders, I've to make you look ill in case anyone from the hotel sees you. If you lie there with your eyes shining like a rainbow, they're not going to believe you're anything but pulsating with good health!"

Vida began to laugh, then she put her fingers over her mouth in case anybody else should hear the sound.

Margit brushed back her hair and tied it at the back of her neck. Then she covered her forehead with a piece of linen, as if she were applying eau de cologne or some other cooling lotion.

She then powdered her face to make her skin look very pale.

"I'm going to send for some tea," she said, "which is all His Highness thinks you should appear to have for breakfast. But I'll order something substantial for myself in my own room, so you will not go hungry."

"I am far too happy to be hungry!"

"I'll be happy when we're out of this pestilential country," Margit said, "and not before!"

She spoke sharply, then walked out of the room, leaving Vida to think.

Even if the Prince's clever plan brought her father out of the monastery in the guise of a Confessor, they still had to escape out of Russia.

Even the Prince could not prevent the Secret Police from catching up with them and apprehending her father, if he had not yet crossed the Hungarian border into safety.

Suddenly her happiness had gone and once again she was desperately anxious.

Perhaps it would be a mistake to bring her father out from the safety of the monastery where he had found sanctuary in the town.

Her only hope now was that, while Vladimir Demidovsky had found out where her father was hiding, the Secret Police might be looking for him elsewhere.

She wished she had asked the Prince more details of what he knew, but she was aware this was not the time for talking to him. That would come later.

Now they had to act, and act quickly.

There was a knock on her door and she guessed it was a maid-servant with her tea.

She therefore shut her eyes and lay back looking, she hoped, very ill with her white face and the linen cloth over her forehead.

The knock came again and now Margit came to the door and she heard her say in Russian:

"Go straight in. Her Ladyship's too ill to speak.

Just put it down by the bed and I'll give it to her in spoonfuls."

Vida heard the maid come in and set down the tea in its samovar.

"Poor lady, so young to be stricken in such a manner," she heard her say.

"It's God's will," Margit said solemnly.

"He always knows best," the maid agreed.

She went from the room and Margit bolted the door behind her.

"Now, sit up and drink," she said. "Later I'll bring you some toast and honey which will at least sustain you until we get out of this place."

"How are we going to do that?" Vida asked.

"His Highness told me he's got a plan for that too. I'm sure we can trust him to think of something clever."

"Yes, we can trust him!" Vida said, a little lilt in her voice.

She drank the tea, then Margit put the samovar outside the door and they waited.

It seemed to Vida as if a century of time passed, although it was actually no more than an hour before there were footsteps on the stairs.

For a minute she was terrified that it might be the Secret Police.

Then the door opened and she first saw Henri, who took a quick glance round the room before he stood back and let a monk enter who had been standing behind him.

At first Vida thought she must be mistaken, then she saw that it was really her father.

She jumped out of bed and flung her arms round his neck.

"Oh, Papa. Papa," she whispered. "It is you! It is really you! Oh, thank God!"

Tears were running down her cheeks and he held her close against him.

Then crying and laughing at the same time, she said:

"I cannot believe that you are here, and dearest Papa, I would never have recognised you with a beard!"

Her father did not answer, but only kissed her. Then he said:

"How could you think of anything so clever, so brilliant, as that I should be your Father Confessor?"

"It was the Prince..." Vida began.

As she spoke there was a very soft knock on the door and Margit drew back the bolt while her father glanced a little nervously over his shoulder and pulled the hood back over his head.

It was the Prince, and he came in to say:

"Thank God we have got you here, Sir Harvey. That at least is a start."

"I might have guessed, Your Highness, that it would be you who would save me!" Sir Harvey said.

"It was also your daughter," the Prince replied.

Even as he smiled at her, Vida realised that when she had jumped out of bed she was wearing only the diaphanous nightgown in which he had seen her the night he had come to her room at the Castle.

Quickly she slipped back under the bed-clothes, and as she did so the Prince said to her father:

"Now, listen to me carefully, because we have very little time. We have to get you well away from Lvov before the abbot realises you will not be returning to the monastery."

"Tell me what is in your mind," Sir Harvey asked.

He spoke quietly, but Vida knew that he was alert and watchful, fully aware of the danger they were in.

At the same time he was facing it with that quiet confidence which came from the power within himself which assured him that he would be successful and survive, however intimidating his enemies might be.

"What I have planned," the Prince began, "and there is not a moment to be lost, is this . . ."

As he started to speak he seemed to Vida to be enveloped with light, and might in fact be St. Michael come down with his angels from Heaven to save them.

chapter five

FORTY minutes later Vida walked out through a side-door into a courtyard to see the Prince's magnificent travelling-carriage drawn by six horses waiting in the sunshine.

She was dressed in the uniform of an outrider, her red hair covered by a white wig and a peaked velvet cap.

She wore a short livery jacket of claret trimmed with gold braid, which was the same as was worn by the servants in the Castle, and below it white buckskin breeches and highly polished boots.

She would have felt embarrassed if any of the five other outriders had looked at her, but as soon as she appeared they mounted the horses which were brought from the stables one by one by the grooms.

Vida was helped onto the saddle of a magnificent Thoroughbred which she knew was of Hungarian origin.

As soon as they were all mounted the carriage drove from the courtyard to the front of the hotel, and the whole cavalcade waited.

Vida held her breath, for she knew this was the most dangerous moment of their deception and that somewhere, although she could not see them, they were being watched by men who would doubtless report to one of the Tzar's Head Agents what was going on.

After several minutes, during which the horses fidgeted and the sun seemed unpleasantly hot on her face, through the door of the hotel came first a shrouded figure in blankets carried by two men, followed by Margit and Henri.

Very carefully the men lifted the shrouded figure onto the back seat of the carriage while Margit, holding a handkerchief, a fan, and various other things that might be required, sat on the seat opposite.

The door of the carriage with its panel painted with the Prince's coat-of-arms was closed, then he himself appeared through the doorway.

Now his black stallion was brought by two grooms to the mounting-block.

The stallion was being extremely obstreperous, rearing and bucking, and the grooms had difficulty in holding it.

As soon as the Prince was in the saddle, the carriage moved away and the outriders rode three on either side of it.

It was only when they passed down the main road of the town and were out into the countryside that

Vida felt she could give a sigh of relief.

When the Prince had expounded his idea that her father should take her place as the woman who was ill and who had come to visit her Confessor, while she herself rode with the outriders, she could hardly believe what she was hearing.

He had taken her agreement to his scheme for granted, and without waiting for her to say anything had gone from the room.

Then almost before she realised what was happening, her father had left her, and Margit was dressing her in the livery which had been brought in to them by the Prince's valet.

"I knew there'd be trouble if we came to Russia," Margit was saying almost beneath her breath.

"Be careful!" Vida begged. "All that matters is that Papa should be safe."

After that they dressed in silence and only when she was ready did Margit, with a sob in her voice, say:

"God go with you, Miss Vida! We need his protection!"

Vida gave her a smile, and walking carefully in boots that were a little too big for her she went down the stairs.

Now, riding astride, she found it surprisingly easy, considering it something she had not done since she was a child.

The carriage was moving very quickly, and causing a cloud of dust to rise behind it.

The outriders therefore took to the fields on either side of the slightly raised road while the Prince rode on ahead of them.

This was not so much by choice, but because his

horse was determined to outstrip anything else on four legs.

For the next three hours all Vida could think of was that her father was moving farther and farther away from the monastery.

Although there might be questions asked as to why he had not returned, they would not be particularly anxious as to his whereabouts until much later in the day.

It was long after noon before they stopped in a clearing in the woods. As she might have expected, the Prince had had their luncheon brought with them.

As Vida dismounted she was wondering whether or not she should stay with the other outriders, when Henri came to her side to say in Russian so that the men would understand:

"His Highness wishes to speak to you."

Vida gave him the reins of her horse, knowing he would know what to do, and walked through the trees to where she saw a table had been set up with some collapsible chairs, and in one of them was seated her father.

The Prince was beside him and Margit had withdrawn into the trees and was sitting alone and out of earshot.

As she reached her father Vida knew that the Prince was watching her and she felt shy that she was wearing breeches.

At the same time, she was well aware it was not a moment for acting modestly when her father's life was at stake.

He must have been wearing his own clothes under the blankets in which he had been carried into the carriage, for now he looked as he always did, very distinguished and, surprisingly, in view of the circumstances, very smart.

His beard had been shaved off and Vida could see that he was much thinner than when she had last seen him.

As this was the first thing that struck her she said:

"You are all right, Papa? Nothing has happened to you?"

She was thinking as she spoke that he might have been tortured or injured in some way.

But he smiled.

"I am quite all right, my dearest. I found however that fish and black bread is not a very sustaining fare for a hungry man."

"That is something I now intend to remedy," the Prince remarked.

As he spoke Vida saw that the outriders who had tied the reins of their horses to the trees so that they could not stray were now bringing luncheon to set it out on the table in front of them.

There was, of course caviar, sturgeon, cold chicken stuffed with pâté de foie gras, and a number of other delicacies which she knew, even without having been half starved as a monk, her father would enjoy.

Then as she wondered if she was expected to stay or, because of the way she was dressed, to help the outriders, the Prince said:

"Sit down, Vida! We have with us specially chosen men whom I can trust with my own life and that of my friends."

Vida gave a little sigh of sheer happiness and sat down beside her father.

"Tell us, Papa, what has happened to you," she begged.

"Later, my dear. For the moment, all I can think of is that I am extremely hungry and I left the monastery before breakfast, which anyway would have been a very meagre meal."

Because she knew him so well she was aware that he was making light of his afflictions.

At the same time, she was terribly afraid because they were still on Russian soil.

"Where are we going?" she asked the Prince.

"We are making for the Hungarian border," he replied, "and tonight we will stay with some friends whom I can trust at Pololia."

"And tomorrow?" Vida queried.

"With luck, we should be in Hungary."

"How can we ever thank you?"

"You can do that when your father is safe," he replied, "but we must not linger. Every moment he is still in Russia constitutes a danger which we would be very foolish to ignore."

"I have been wondering ever since I reached the comparative safety of the monastery," Sir Harvey said, "how I could possibly let you know where I was hiding."

"You have given me many anxious nights and days of worry," the Prince said quietly.

"I did not dare to trust the Abbot," Sir Harvey said. "He had been personally appointed by the Tzar, and there were several monks who were unpleasantly curious about me."

"They will know their curiosity was justified when you do not return," the Prince remarked dryly, "so the sooner we are on our way the better!"

Having drunk several glasses of golden wine, Sir Harvey looked more like his old self and Vida said:

"I love you, Papa! I do not think I could ever bear to go through this agony again."

"You are right, my dearest," Sir Harvey agreed. "This has been my swan-song as far as Russia is concerned, but I think the Marquess of Salisbury will be delighted by what I have to tell him."

There was no time to say any more because the Prince who had moved away to speak to his men came back to say:

"Vida will now travel inside the carriage, and her horse will be ridden by the footman who was on the box."

He smiled at Vida, then he said:

"When we arrive at Pololia you will be not your father's daughter, but I will introduce you by the name on your passport. We must not make any foolish mistakes, just in case we are interrogated."

"And Papa?" Vida asked.

"Your father is an old Hungarian friend whom we are taking back to his own country and his passport is in the name of your mother's family."

"The Rákŏczis!" Vida exclaimed.

"Exactly!" the Prince agreed.

The outriders had already whisked the table and chairs away and as Margit rejoined them from beneath the trees, Vida followed by her father stepped inside the carriage.

As soon as it moved, Margit produced Vida's clothes from a sheet in which she had wrapped them, explaining that Sir Harvey had carried them on his lap so that they would not be seen by anybody watching him being conveyed from the hotel into the carriage.

"It was His Highness's idea! He thinks of everything!" Margit said proudly.

While Sir Harvey buried himself in a newspaper Vida took off the clothes in which she had ridden as an outrider and dressed herself in a very pretty gown which Margit had chosen for her.

There was a small travelling-bonnet to put on her head, but she decided it would be uncomfortable, as they still had a long way to go.

Instead, she merely let Margit arrange her red hair as she always wore it.

Later, because the Prince had said she was to appear as the Countess Kărólzi, she made up her face, and her father watched with amusement.

"You certainly chose a very alluring disguise, my dearest," he said. "I am not surprised the Prince finds you beautiful and pressed you to stay on as his guest."

"I stayed because I thought only by doing so would I find out whether or not he was to be trusted," Vida said.

"I was very remiss in not telling you before I went on this wild trip," Sir Harvey said, "that the Prince is a very old friend and somebody with whom I have worked for many years."

"I wish I had known that before."

"I did not tell you," her father explained, "simply because I never dreamt for one moment that you would come in search of me. And as you well know, in this game the less anyone else knows the better."

"I know that is right, Papa. At the same time, I was terribly afraid that if I trusted the Prince you might be in worse danger than you were already."

She told her father how Vladimir Demidovsky had spoken to her in Budapest, and then how after she had seen him going into the Prince's bedroom she had been certain that His Highness was not to be trusted.

She had therefore felt she must leave the Castle immediately.

"I quite understand how it happened," her father said, "and it was very brave of you, my dearest. But I cannot bear to think of your being involved in a situation which might have turned out very differently."

"We are not safe yet," Vida said with a little tremor in her voice.

"I know," Sir Harvey agreed. "At the same time, Lady Luck has always been on my side, and I cannot believe she will fail me now."

"I am sure she will not!"

Even so, Vida felt a little tremor go through her almost as if it were a warning not to be overconfident.

She talked to her father during the afternoon while Margit slept peacefully opposite them.

There was so much she wanted to tell him, so much she wanted to hear.

While he was reticent about his adventures, she did learn that as soon as he entered Russia he had quickly become aware that he was being followed.

After some close shaves when he was nearly captured by the Tzar's Secret Police, he had, in desperation, entered the monastery as a travelling monk.

He had told the Abbot he was on his way to Odessa, but felt too ill to go any farther.

The Abbot had believed his story and after he had

been nursed back to health had begged him not to hurry on his journey but to stay in the monastery for as long as he wished.

"That was fortunate for you, Papa."

"It was fortunate that I was still there when you and His Highness arrived," Sir Harvey said, "but I was beginning to find an enclosed life of continual prayer very restricting."

Vida laughed.

"I am sure you hated every moment of it."

"I missed my creature comforts," Sir Harvey admitted, "and of course you, my beloved daughter."

"As I missed you, Papa."

One thing Vida had not told her father was how the Prince had come to her bedroom, believing her story that she was a widow and intending to make love to her.

She felt it would upset him and make him angry, when she herself was so grateful to the Prince that she had no wish to do anything but praise him.

She loved listening to Margit now extolling his virtues, when previously the old maid had been so suspicious.

She wondered what had happened to his other guests at the Castle and thought it was something she must ask him when there was a chance of their being alone together and not in a hurry.

They arrived at Pololia when the sun had lost its warmth, and it was in fact growing late.

The horses might not be very tired, but owing to the dust and the heat Vida was certain they were thirsty, as she was.

She had hoped the Prince might stop for a little while during the afternoon, but she was sure he had his own reasons to keep going and that they were good ones.

Pololia was a small town, little larger than a village.

Overlooking it on a low hill with trees protecting it from the north was a large house.

It was not a Castle, but it was certainly old and was sturdily built, as if at one time it had been a fortification of some sort.

Vida realised that the Prince had sent one of his outriders ahead to alert the owner of their arrival.

Because of the speed at which they had travelled, however, he could not have been more than half an hour ahead of them.

Nevertheless they received a very warm welcome from an elderly man with white hair and his wife, who was considerably younger than he was.

It was quite obvious to Vida from the way she looked at the Prince and the way she talked to him that she found him extremely attractive.

Vida therefore felt glad that she was dressed once again as a Countess and was wearing a gown that might have belonged to any of the beautiful women among the Prince's guests at the Castle.

She was given a large, comfortable bedroom on the first floor, with her father in the room next door.

The Prince was on the other side of the corridor and, although the house was not in any way as grand as his Castle, there were plenty of servants to wait on them.

What Vida enjoyed more than anything else was that she could have a bath.

After she had soaked in the scented water for some time she said to Margit:

"Now I feel better! This will be a very exciting

adventure to tell my children someday, if I have any!"

"We're not out of the wood yet, Miss Vida," Margit said.

She spoke in English, and as if her words made her realise they were still in Russia, Vida said quickly:

"Be careful!"

Margit put her hand up to her lips.

"I keep forgetting," she said. "All I can think of is thanking God that the master is with us."

"That is what I have been doing," Vida said with a smile. "But remember, Margit, I am a Countess, and not until tomorrow in Hungary can I be myself."

She spoke in a whisper while concentrating on her face before she went down to dinner.

There was fortunately nobody else staying in the house, and the dinner was a delicious meal of good food, good wine, and stimulating conversation.

The Prince made them laugh with stories of his travels in different parts of the world, and some of the strange characters he had met in Monte Carlo.

But he was very careful, Vida noticed, not to talk about the Tzar or St. Petersburg, or even of what was happening in his own Castle.

"We live very quietly here," his hostess said, "and I cannot tell you how thrilling it is, Your Highness, to be able to entertain you."

"I have been very remiss not to have paid you a visit for the past five years," he replied, "but as soon as I return home you must both come to stay with me."

Her excitement at the invitation and the expression in her eyes told Vida all too clearly what she was feeling.

She suddenly thought that the sensations the Prince had aroused in her were probably felt by every woman he met, and therefore to him must be very commonplace.

Fortunately the lights in the Dining-Room were dim, for she was finding it difficult to smile, let alone laugh.

'He makes love to every woman who attracts him,' she told herself, 'and when he has left us in Hungary I do not suppose we shall ever see him again.'

As she went up to bed there was a heavy feeling in her breast, as if there were a stone there.

It persisted even after she had kissed her father good night and had said over and over again how happy she was to know that he was sleeping in the next room.

"I am looking forward to a comfortable bed," Sir Harvey said. "I assure you the monks have a pallet that is as rough and stony as the path to Heaven!"

Vida laughed.

"Oh, Papa, I promise you that from now on you shall always have a feather-bed which will be as comfortable as a cloud."

"I shall be looking forward to it," her father replied.

He kissed Vida again and said:

"I am very touched and very proud, my darling, of what you have done to save me. But it is something I will never let you undertake again."

"Then you must not get into trouble, Papa, otherwise you know I shall always attempt to rescue you, however difficult it may seem."

"Now you are definitely blackmailing me!" Sir Harvey protested.

He kissed her once again before he went to his own room.

Vida sent Margit to bed because the old maid looked very tired.

She undressed herself, brushed her hair until it seemed to dance with an electricity of its own, then wearing one of her pretty lace-trimmed nightgowns she slipped between the cool linen sheets.

* * *

Vida was so tired after such a long day of combined fear and excitement that she fell asleep immediately, and only awoke when her father came into the room.

He was wearing a silk dressing-gown which he had obviously borrowed from the Prince, and he said:

"It is still very early, my dearest, but I know the Prince intends that we should leave immediately after breakfast, and I wanted to have a talk with you first."

"What about, Papa?"

Her father sat down beside the bed and said as if he were a little embarrassed:

"Well, actually, it is about His Highness."

Vida sat up, patting the pillows up behind her.

There was a little silence, then he began:

"You are very young, Vida, and although we have done many things together and travelled in a lot of different countries, I know that you have never met a man like Prince Ivan Pavolivski before, for the simple reason that he is unique."

"That is what I thought, Papa."

"But because he is unique, because he is one of the most intelligent, as well as one of the most handsome men I have ever seen," Sir Harvey went on, "I do not want you to lose your heart."

It was not what Vida had expected him to say, and as she looked at her father in surprise, she was annoyed to feel the colour coming into her cheeks.

"And you think that . . . is what I might do . . . ?" she asked defensively.

"Yes, because it is what happens with every woman the Prince meets," her father said.

He gave a little sigh before he continued.

"There is something magnetic about him. He is a Pied Piper, and I have never known a woman who did not find him irresistible."

That was what Vida had thought herself, but she had no wish to admit it.

"I was thinking only last night, Papa, that it is very unlikely that we shall ever see His Highness after we reach Hungary today, as we hope."

"That is what I myself expect," Sir Harvey replied. "But it is quite obvious to me that Prince Ivan admires you, and therefore I can only beg you, my dearest, to remember he is a will-o'-the-wisp, a man who will sweep into your life like a meteor passing through the sky, and disappear just as quickly."

There was a worried note in Sir Harvey's voice which Vida thought was rather touching.

"I understand exactly what you are saying, Papa," she said, "and I promise I will not only be on my guard, but will make quite certain that I recognise the Prince for what he is."

There was a little pause before Sir Harvey said:

"I know you will not mind my saying this to you, my dearest. It is, after all, what your mother would say to you if she were alive. But I could not bear, after all we have been to each other, that you should be unhappy over a man who never in any circumstances could mean anything in your life."

"Of course not, Papa," Vida agreed. "He is Russian, and one place I will never visit again is Russia!"

She thought as she spoke that they might meet the Prince in Monte Carlo, Paris, or perhaps London, then told herself that was irrelevant.

Her father was right; he was a meteor flashing past them, and the sooner she forgot the sensations he aroused in her the better.

But at the back of her mind was a question she could not dismiss, which was:

'How will you forget the first kiss you ever received?'

Having said what he had come to say, Sir Harvey started to talk of other things, suggesting to Vida that they might visit her mother's relatives when they had crossed the border into Hungary.

"I think, Papa, that is a wonderful idea . . . !" Vida was saying when suddenly the door opened and to her surprise the Prince came into the room.

One look at the expression on his face made the words she was saying die on her lips.

"The Secret Police are here," he said in a low voice. "Get into the wardrobe, Sir Harvey!"

There was a large carved wardrobe on one wall of the room and with the swiftness of a man who was used to facing danger, Sir Harvey moved across the room almost before the words had been spoken, and disappeared inside it.

Then to Vida's astonishment the Prince threw off

the silk robe he was wearing and even as there was the sound of footsteps in the passage outside he got into bed beside her.

Before she could even look at the Prince, let alone ask what he was doing, his arms went round her and he pulled her close against him.

As the door opened his lips came down on hers.

At first she was terrified at what was happening. Then as she felt the hard pressure of the Prince's mouth, and the closeness of his body, she was more vividly aware of him than of the danger they were in.

It must have been only the passing of a few seconds, and yet it seemed like an interminable passage of time before, as if the Prince were suddenly conscious there was somebody in the room, he raised his head and looked towards the door.

Standing in the doorway were three men, and as Vida looked at them too she thought that if she had seen them anywhere she would have suspected they were Secret Agents.

With their sharp features, their thin lips, and their suspicious eyes they might, in fact, have stepped out of a caricature.

Without taking his arms from around Vida the Prince said in Russian as if he were both astonished and angry:

"What the devil do you think you are doing, coming in here?"

As the man who was standing in front of the two others advanced towards the bed he obviously recognised the Prince.

"Your Highness!" he exclaimed.

"Never mind that," the Prince said. "Let me ask

you again why you are bursting, in this astonishing way, into a private bedroom in a private house?"

"We are looking for a man, Your Highness."

"I guessed as much," the Prince replied, "but as you can see he is not here, kindly conduct your investigations somewhere else!"

Almost as if the Prince had told her what to do, the moment he had begun speaking Vida had hidden her face against his shoulder, as if she were shy.

All the Secret Agents could see was that she was in the Prince's arms, they were in bed together, and her red hair was falling over her shoulders.

"I am sorry, Your Highness," the man in the doorway said apologetically, "but we were informed that a man we are seeking was here with a lady who had been taken ill."

"Well, you are mistaken!" the Prince said.

"I realise that now, and please forgive us, Your Highness."

"There is no other man in my party except for my own servants for whom I can vouch, and Count Rákŏczi, an old friend whom I am conveying to his house in Hungary. He has his papers with him, if you wish to see them."

"There is no need, Your Highness," the man replied. "We are not seeking a Hungarian."

"Very well," the Prince said, "and perhaps now we can be left alone."

The man who had been speaking glanced at Vida with a faint smile on his thin lips.

Only when he would have withdrawn, one of the men behind him bent to whisper something into his ear.

Instantly he turned and said:

"Excuse me, Your Highness."

The Prince was already looking down at Vida as if he had forgotten the whole episode, and looked up again.

"What is it now?" he asked irritably. "Really, I should have thought you could have had a little more tact!"

"I can only apologise once again, Your Highness, but I had forgotten something very important."

"What is it?" the Prince asked impatiently.

"We received instructions from our superior last night that if, as was rumoured, you were somewhere in the vicinity, we were to give Your Highness a message from His Imperial Majesty the Tzar."

"A message?" the Prince asked. "Then why was I not given it at once?"

"We—we did not expect to find you here, Your Highness," the man stammered, "and it had therefore slipped my memory."

"What is the message?"

"His Imperial Majesty is in Kiev, and he asks that Your Highness will proceed there immediately and bring with you the Countess Kărólzi who has been staying with you at your Castle."

The Prince did not reply and the man went on.

"I understand, Your Highness, that somebody has already gone to your Castle in order to convey the message to you, and to any other place where you are likely to be."

"Thank you," the Prince said. "Inform your superior that I shall certainly obey His Imperial Majesty's command and be with him as soon as is humanly possible."

"I thank Your Highness."

The man bowed low, and the two men behind him also bowed.

Then the door was shut, but the Prince did not move.

Vida knew, because his whole body was stiff, that he was listening intently and she did not speak but listened too.

After what seemed a long time there was just the faint sound of footsteps moving away from the door.

Still Sir Harvey did not come from the wardrobe.

It was only after the Prince had got out of bed and put on his robe that he exclaimed:

"This is intolerable! Completely intolerable!"

It was then that the wardrobe opened and Sir Harvey stepped out into the room saying as he did so:

"It was fortunate, Your Highness, that you saw those men arriving."

"As they did not ask to see you," the Prince said, "I think they were satisfied, but one never knows."

"They were obviously not the same men who might have been watching us at Lvov."

"No, I realise that," the Prince said. "At the same time, their report will go back to their superior as you heard, and we must take no chances of your being interrogated before you leave the country."

"Oh, please," Vida cried, "we must get him away, we cannot . . . lose him now!"

The Prince looked at her, then he said:

"There is only one way we can make certain that he is safe."

"What is that?" Vida asked.

"That you come with me to Kiev. If I go alone, having received what is virtually an Imperial order, they will be sure there is something suspicious, not only about your father, but also about you."

"I see no reason..." Sir Harvey began.

Then he paused and added:

"Yes, of course, you are right. Vida is supposed to be Russian, and is therefore not interested in your Hungarian friend."

There was a silence as all three were thinking over what had been said, and it was Vida who spoke first.

"Then of course I must come to Kiev with you," she said to the Prince, "if by doing so I can ensure that Papa escapes into Hungary."

The Prince walked across the room to stand at the window.

Vida knew he was thinking, and after a moment looking down below him he said:

"The three men are leaving in a *troika* drawn by two horses. It will, I hope, take them some time to reach their superior, whoever he may be. You, Sir Harvey, must be over the border before there is any chance of their thinking they should have seen you before they left."

"I understand," Sir Harvey said.

"The quickest way, of course, would be to ride. Do you think that would be too much for you?"

Sir Harvey's eyes twinkled.

"No worse, I imagine, than a hard day's hunting."

The Prince laughed.

"Very well. I will send you on one of my best and fastest horses accompanied by two of my men who are, I assure you, crack shots in an emergency. If you travel as the crow flies, you will be in Hungary far quicker than by following the road which from here twists and turns, and is especially hard-going when you reach the mountains."

"I will go to get ready," Sir Harvey said, "and I trust you with Vida who, as you know, is very precious to me."

"As soon as we have paid our respects to the Tzar," the Prince said, "we will return to the Castle. From there I will take her to Sarospatak."

Sir Harvey nodded.

"I will wait until I hear you are over the border with the Răkóczis. They are very hospitable and will, I know, welcome me as their guest."

"Then that is settled," the Prince said, "and for God's sake hurry! Vida and I will make our way leisurely towards the nearest railway station."

He went from the room as he spoke without saying any more and Vida was left alone to lie back against the pillows, feeling it was impossible to realise what had happened, or what the future held.

She was however so frightened for her father that she felt that nothing else was really important.

At the same time, she could not help feeling a thrill that she would not be leaving the Prince today as she had expected, but would still be with him for a few more days, perhaps even longer.

"I must remember what Papa said to me," she told herself, but she knew it was going to be difficult.

She had only just begun to dress and was sitting in front of the dressing-table with her hair still falling over her shoulders when Sir Harvey came back into her room.

He was wearing the ordinary clothes of a gentleman going riding, and she jumped to her feet, ran to him, and put her arms around his neck.

"Promise me, Papa," she said, "that you will ride as quickly as possible, for only when you cross safely into Hungary will the Tzar's men be unable to harm you."

"That is what I intend to do," Sir Harvey said. "It would be a terrible waste of your and the Prince's efforts if I failed you both now."

"I am sure Mama is looking after you," Vida said in a soft voice, "and you know I shall be praying for your safety."

"I am only ashamed of having got you into this mess," her father replied. "But His Highness is right: it would not only look suspicious if you travel with me instead of with him, but it would certainly slow me down, and I can go faster on my own."

"I will join you as quickly as I can," Vida promised, "and then, Papa, we will never come back again to this horrible and menacing country."

She drew in her breath before she asked:

"How is it possible that the Secret Police can burst into private rooms without permission?"

"That is the least of what they do," her father said, "but we will talk about it another time. I must go now, my dearest."

"You have everything you want?"

"Everything except you," he answered. "Take very great care of yourself, and do exactly what His Highness tells you. He is clever enough to be the Tzar's 'pet,' so you will come to no harm there."

"No, of course not," Vida agreed.

Sir Harvey kissed her, then as he left her room she heard him speaking to someone outside the door and knew that the Prince was seeing him off.

She went to the window and a few minutes later she saw her father riding away from the main doorway on what she was sure was the magnificent stallion which the Prince had been riding yesterday.

She knew that her father was a very experienced horseman who would enjoy being mounted on such a fine animal.

The two men accompanying him were also riding horses which she was sure would outpace anything on four legs in the whole vicinity.

"Unless the Secret Police have wings, they will not catch up with Papa," she said to Margit, who had joined her at the window.

"Don't tempt fate, it's unlucky!" Margit replied.

Vida watched him anxiously. Then when the three figures had vanished into the misty distance, she went back to the dressing-table.

"I now have to meet the Tzar," she said aloud.

But even as she spoke she knew her heart was saying something very different.

In fact, it was telling her that she would be with the Prince, and that was what she wanted wildly, insistently, although she was afraid to admit it.

chapter six

WHEN Vida had eaten her breakfast, which was brought
to her room, and was dressed ready for travelling, she
went downstairs.

The Prince, who had breakfasted with his hosts,
was waiting for her and she did not miss the way in
which their pretty hostess was hanging on his words
and repeating several times how much she was looking
forward to coming to stay at the Castle.

The Prince kissed her hand in a graceful manner
which Vida thought could not be equalled by a man
of any other nationality except a Frenchman.

Then having again warmly thanked his hosts for
their hospitality he helped Vida into the carriage.

She had expected that Margit would sit opposite
them, as she had done on the previous day, but to her
surprise another carriage was produced in which

Margit, Henri, and the Prince's valet travelled.

With them was carried what seemed to be an enormous amount of luggage belonging to the Prince.

Vida realised that he would need special clothes to wear when they met the Tzar, and she only hoped that she would not let him down in the gowns she had brought with her to Russia.

As they drove off he turned a little sideways against the soft cushions of his carriage and said:

"Well, Vida, I said *we* would save your father, and that, I think, is what *we* have done."

"You mean *you* have saved him," Vida corrected. "If you had not been aware that those men had arrived this morning, it might have been disastrous."

"But it did give me an opportunity," the Prince said softly, "to hold you in my arms."

When she remembered how he had kissed her she felt herself blush.

Then she knew she was being very foolish to think of what had been an emergency action as something intimate and personal.

As if the Prince were reading her thoughts he said:

"You are very lovely, and I think that I like you best when you are young, innocent, and untouched."

He emphasised the words and Vida blushed again.

She did not know what to say, and after a moment the Prince went on.

"I realise now that you came to the Castle deliberately to captivate me, and it was a clever idea. At the same time, I think it would have been more intelligent from the point of view of intrigue, if you had come as yourself."

"How could I do that," Vida asked indignantly,

"when I had no idea it would be safe for me to come as Papa's daughter? It might have made things more dangerous for him than they were already."

"Of course you could not know," the Prince said, "and so you bewildered and intrigued me and, as you intended, captivated me."

Vida felt her heart leap at what he was saying.

At the same time she remembered the warning her father had given her, and told herself he was only flirting with her as he would flirt with any pretty woman in the circumstances.

Because she was frightened of the way he made her feel, she tried to change the subject.

"Tell me about the country through which we are now passing," she said. "I know it is the Ukraine, which I have always understood is considerably different from the rest of Russia."

"That is true," the Prince agreed. "All through our history the Ukrainians have had very distinguishing features and, of course, their own language."

Knowing she was genuinely interested, he told her how it was in Kiev, where they were to meet the Tzar, that Christianity had made its first foothold in Russia.

The Prince of Kiev had had his people collectively baptised in the Dnieper River in A.D. 908.

Because history had always interested Vida she listened to him as attentively as a child hearing a fairy-story, and as they travelled on, the Prince pointed out to her the wooded steppes planted with oak and beech trees.

Later they came to the treeless zone, with its fertile black soil.

Because the Prince was like a genie, able to conjure

up everything he wanted with a wave of his hand, Vida was not surprised when they arrived at a railway station to find waiting for them the Prince's own train, which was to carry them to Kiev.

They had stopped for luncheon at an attractive hostelry in a small town, and a private room had been ordered for the Prince by one of the outriders who had gone ahead.

Then they ate his own food and drank his own wine, which was, Vida was sure, very different from what an ordinary passing traveller would have been offered.

It was so exciting to be alone with the Prince and be able to talk to him and see his dark, penetrating eyes looking into hers, that after a very short while she told herself that warning or no warning, she might as well enjoy herself while she had the opportunity.

She tried to remember not to be so foolish as to think that the Prince meant anything serious by the compliments he paid her, or by the beguiling manner in which he spoke, which despite every resolution made her heart turn over in her breast.

'He is the Pied Piper, as Papa said,' she thought, 'and why should I be the only one to ignore his music?'

So she let herself listen, and it was very hard, even though she knew it was wrong, not to long for him to hold her close to him and kiss her again.

She had only to think of those moments when his kisses had swept her up to the stars, to feel again the fire he had kindled in her and the sensations that were different from anything she had ever imagined flying from her heart to her lips.

'I am making a fool of myself,' she thought as luncheon ended.

As the Prince sat down beside her again in the carriage, he put out his hand to tuck in the rug which had been placed over her knees a little more firmly, and she felt herself thrill.

Now the carriage was open and she knew it was because the Prince felt that the whole world, as far as he was concerned, could see them.

He was merely doing his duty in obeying the Tzar.

She thought too, although it was best not to say so, that he felt that by now her father would be nearing the border.

Unless something very untoward happened, in two or three hours he would reach Hungary and be on his way to the Rǎkóczi Castle.

As if the Prince knew what she was thinking, even when she had not spoken, which was one of the disconcerting things about him, he said:

"Do not worry. I know with my sixth sense that your father will reach safety."

"That is the sense I also try to use," Vida said, "but sometimes I cannot help fearing it may mislead me."

"It certainly did not guide you rightly where I was concerned," the Prince said quietly.

She felt he was accusing her and after a moment she answered:

"I really did want to trust you, and I swear that I was almost convinced I could do so until I saw Vladimir Demidovsky going into your bedroom."

"He should not have made you suspicious by the way he spoke to you in Budapest," the Prince said. "In fact, I shall rebuke him for doing so."

"Perhaps if I had been an ordinary traveller with nothing to conceal," Vida said, "I should have simply thought he was trying to take advantage of a woman travelling alone. As it was, for Papa's sake, I was frightened of everybody."

"You are being generous," the Prince answered, "but I expect perfection in anything that concerns me."

Vida gave a little laugh.

"How often are you disappointed?"

"Very often," he answered, "especially where women are concerned."

She looked at him enquiringly and he put his hand over hers.

"Do not disappoint me," he said. "I find everything about you almost too perfect to be real, and as yet, there are no flaws."

"You are asking too much."

"Am I?"

She had no answer to this and she looked away from him at the fertile countryside through which they were passing, and an hour later they arrived at Kishineu.

The Prince's train was everything she might have expected.

It was painted white and red, and displayed the Prince's coat-of-arms just as on the doors of his horse-drawn carriages.

The attendants wore his claret and gold livery.

The Dining-Room Car was magnificently furnished, and the bedroom in which Vida was to sleep because they would not arrive in Kiev until the next day was, although small, very luxurious.

The coach-work consisted of a blending of woods of local trees, painted and decorated in an unusual and attractive manner.

The upholstery of the chairs and the curtains that

hung at the sides of the windows were of velvet.

"It is so lovely," Vida exclaimed, "that I feel you could live in it!"

The Prince smiled.

"I have too many houses to make that requirement necessary."

"The trouble with you," she said provocatively, "is that you are spoilt! Your Highness has everything you could ask for. I thought just now you are like a genie to whom one has only to make a wish for it to be granted."

"That is what I feel about you," he replied. "I have wished for you for a long time. Now, when I had almost given up hope, you are here."

It was a very pretty speech, but Vida thought she was not to take it seriously.

At the same time, again her heart was turning over, but she was saved from making a reply because as the train started, the servants brought in caviar and champagne, even though it was not long since they had had luncheon.

There was much of interest to see from the windows as they steamed towards Kiev.

But Vida found it hard to look at anything except the Prince's handsome face, or to hear anything but the music of his deep voice.

They changed for dinner just as they would have done if they had been staying in his Castle.

Margit would have taken one of Vida's elaborate and sensational gowns from her trunk, but she shook her head.

"Give me one of my own," she said. "A white one!"

Margit looked at her in surprise and she said:

"Tonight I want to be myself. Tomorrow when we arrive at Kiev I will be the Countess Kărólzi."

"I don't know what your mother would say about these goings-on!" Margit remarked. "The Prince is a fine gentleman and I'm not saying any different, and it's a miracle the way he saved the master. But you know as well as I do, Miss Vida, that you should have a chaperone with you!"

"I dare say when we arrive in Kiev His Majesty the Tzar will prove a very effective one," Vida answered lightly.

"Now, listen to me, Miss Vida," Margit said in the tone of a scolding nanny. "You watch your step where His Highness is concerned. He can account for more broken hearts than most sportsmen can tot up their pheasants, and I've no wish for you to be one of them!"

Vida felt a pang of jealousy at what Margit had said and wanted to reply that it was too late! For the Prince had already captured her heart as he had captured so many others.

At the same time, she was still fighting to keep control of her own feelings.

She was trying with an almost superhuman effort not to be mesmerised by his charm, the compliments he paid her, and the fire in his dark eyes.

'I have to remember,' she warned herself when she was dressed, 'that when this dream-world comes to an end, I shall have to go back to the reality of a normal life, and never see the Prince again.'

When she went into the Drawing-Room car, where he was waiting for her, she knew by his expression when he saw her that all she wanted was to please him.

No amount of common sense could prevent her from feeling as if he lifted her into the sky.

In her white gown, with only a touch of powder on her flawless skin, and her only ornamentation a white rose from the flowers arranged in her sleeping-car, she looked very young and very lovely.

The Prince rose as she walked towards him and when she reached him he said in a low voice:

"Now you have stepped straight out of my dreams. This is how I have seen you in my heart for many years."

Vida wanted to reply that she too had dreamt of him! But he was so much more wonderful than any "Dream-Lover" she could have imagined, that she could only look at him wide-eyed.

She thought that no man could be so handsome, so incredibly attractive.

They sat down side by side on a sofa, were served with the usual glass of champagne and delicious canapes.

Dinner was brought to them and served with a style and expertise that was part of his insistence on perfection.

Afterwards Vida found it impossible to remember what she had eaten or drunk, or even what they had talked about.

She was only conscious that the Prince was close to her, and his vibrations were so strong that she felt as if she could not only feel them, but positively see them.

When after the meal was over, the table in front of them had been cleared away, and they were alone, the Prince said:

"You have had a long day, my dearest heart, and

I am going to send you to bed early because I want you to look very beautiful when we arrive at Kiev tomorrow."

"At what time do we arrive?" Vida asked, a little tremor in her voice.

She was afraid he would reply first thing in the morning, but instead with a smile he answered:

"I do not think either of us wants to spend more time than is necessary with His Imperial Majesty, and as the food at his Palaces is always indescribably unpleasant, I have arranged for us to have an early luncheon here before we see the Royal Presence."

Because Vida was curious, she asked why the food at the Palaces was so unpleasant.

"The Tzar is frugal to the point of miserliness," the Prince explained. "Since his accession he has cut down on entertaining and made stringent economies on food and wine. He has issued orders that soap and candles must be used as fully as possible before they are thrown away, and the table linen is not to be changed every day."

Vida laughed.

"It does not seem possible."

"It is true," the Prince said, "and the Tzar's favourite food is cabbage and gruel! Although he does not inflict these dishes on his guests, anybody who stays at the Gatshina Palace always complains that the food is inedible."

"It is unbelievable!" Vida said, thinking of the enormous wealth of the Russian Grand Dukes and their wild extravagance when they travelled around Europe.

"The best thing we can do," the Prince continued,

"is to eat all we need before we join the Tzar, and expect a dinner that is best left alone."

"Surely it is not in one of his own Palaces that His Imperial Majesty is staying in Kiev?" Vida asked.

"No, it belongs to the Prince of Kiev. He is a generous man, but like any other subject who entertains the Emperor of all the Russias, he is not so foolish as to flaunt his wealth."

Vida gave a little laugh.

"What you are saying is that if he did, he might be taxed even more heavily than he is already!"

It was the Prince's turn to laugh.

"I can see not only do you understand what is happening in Russia, but you realise that things are different in every way from when Alexander II, who was a kindly man, was on the throne."

Vida was going to ask him to tell her about Alexander II, when he added:

"He was both human and understanding because he was in love. He loved someone very dearly, and their romance was like something out of a novel."

"Papa told me about it once," Vida answered.

She longed to ask the Prince if that was the sort of love he was looking for in his life.

Then she remembered that Tzar Alexander II had had a wife who was jealous and miserable because of his love for his mistress.

It was something Vida did not wish to discuss at the moment, and she said quickly:

"Tell me more about the Tzar I am to meet tomorrow. Will he frighten me?"

"He frightens most people," the Prince said wryly, "including me!"

"I thought you were frightened of nothing and nobody!" Vida teased.

"I am when it concerns the Tzar," the Prince said seriously, "because he is very unpredictable."

He was silent for a moment. Then he said:

"I have painted a gloomy picture which is perhaps a little biased. Like his grandfather, the Tzar is devoted to his wife and children, five of them, and is unfailingly kind to all the members of his family."

Vida thought this was cold comfort when one remembered the horrors the Tzar had perpetrated on the Jews, and on any other of his subjects who had incurred his displeasure.

She did not however feel it was safe to say so, and instead she asked the Prince to tell her about her relatives, the Räkóczis, whom he knew far better than she did.

"I know they will be delighted to see your father," the Prince said.

Then with perception that was characteristic of him he added:

"I know you are tired, even though you are pretending otherwise. You have had a difficult day, but by this time your father is safe, and you can sleep peacefully and no longer be afraid."

Because she felt she must do as he said Vida rose to her feet, and the Prince rose too and said:

"Good night, my Dream-Comé-True. When we are travelling in a different direction from where we are going now, I shall have a great deal to say to you. But let us take our fences one at a time."

Vida smiled at him, then his arms were round her and he pulled her close against him.

For a moment he looked down at her face as if he were engraving it on his memory. Then he asked:

"How can you be so beautiful with at the same time so much more to you than the beauty that lies on the surface? It is as if your heart speaks to my heart, your soul to my soul, and I know I can never lose you."

He did not wait for an answer but his lips were on hers.

As the rapture and ecstasy of his kisses carried Vida up into the stars she knew that nothing anybody could say could prevent her from loving the Prince.

However foolish it might be, her heart was at his feet.

* * *

The Prince's train was shunted into a siding outside the station at Kiev just before noon and they lunched on sturgeon that had been caught in the Dnieper River that morning.

There were also other dishes that were different from anything they had been served before.

When she asked how this was possible, the Prince said that the Chef he kept on the train had been to the market to purchase anything that he thought would please them.

"I am enjoying every mouthful," Vida said.

"I think what I adore about you more than anything else," the Prince replied, "is that, so unlike me, you are completely unspoilt."

She gave a little laugh, and he added:

"How could you suppose that anybody would take

you for a sophisticated woman of twenty-three, when you enjoy everything like a schoolgirl? When your laughter is as young as the song of the birds when dawn breaks?"

"You say such lovely and poetical things to me!" Vida said. "I want to write them down and keep them, so that when I am old I shall be able to read them and remember this moment."

"There will be other moments for you to remember, my precious," the Prince replied. "But now the carriage is waiting, and we had better make our way to the Palace and hope His Imperial Majesty is in a good temper!"

The way the Prince spoke made Vida feel a little apprehensive.

Then she told herself it was not important whether she liked or disliked the Tzar.

He would mean nothing in her life, however much the Prince, being a Russian, had to kow-tow to him.

She remembered how her father had said that the Prince was the Tzar's pet, and she thought it was extremely clever of him to have managed to now pull the wool over His Imperial Majesty's eyes.

The Tzar could have no suspicion that the Prince was helping people like her father and, she suspected, many of the Jews who had been driven so cruelly and despicably from Russia without being allowed to take their own possessions with them.

The Palace was old and had been partly rebuilt by every new Prince of Kiev who had inherited it since the Kievian period of Russian history.

As they drove towards it Vida realised that the town lay on both sides of the Dnieper River, where on the left bank the ground was hilly while on the right was an extensive flat plain.

"Kiev is one of the most interesting cities in our country," the Prince said as they drove along. "In the Chronicles it is described as the 'Mother of Russian Cities.'"

"It is certainly very attractive," Vida said.

When they reached the Palace it was impossible to think of anything but what lay ahead.

Soon they were walking along corridors with walls that might have stood there since the twelfth century, until they reached the door of a very impressive room.

It was flung open by a flunkey who intoned in a stentorian voice:

"His Highness Prince Ivan Pavolivski and the Countess Vida Kărólzi!"

It was then, as the Prince of Kiev advanced to greet them from the far end of the room, that she had her first glimpse of His Imperial Majesty, Emperor of all the Russias, Alexander III.

Her father had told her that Alexander was a giant of a man, and very proud of his physical strength.

"He can tear a pack of cards in half," Sir Harvey had said, "bend an iron poker over his knees, and crush a silver rouble with his bare hands."

Vida laughed and said:

"Not very useful attributes in an Emperor!"

Yet now as she looked at him she realised they were symbolic of the strength and cruelty of a man who terrorised the country over which he ruled.

He was only forty-two, but he was already growing bald, his eyes were expressionless, and he moved in a particularly ungainly fashion.

Although almost every drop of blood in his veins was German, Alexander had the stubborn and enigmatic look of a Russian peasant.

But now as he greeted Prince Ivan he was smiling, and only when the Prince presented Vida and she sank down in a very low curtsy did his expression change, and she felt there was a cruel twist to his lips which she did not understand.

The Prince of Kiev, a youngish man who was obviously very eager to be pleasant, asked Prince Ivan about their journey.

"I came as soon as I received His Imperial Majesty's command," the Prince said.

He looked at the Tzar as if for approval, and as he did so somebody came into the room behind them. Vida immediately realised that it was the Princess Eudoxia, whom she had met at the Castle.

She was looking very beautiful, even more beautiful, Vida thought, than when she had last seen her.

She was dressed not only very elegantly in a French gown, but there were several ropes of large pearls around her neck, and pearls hanging from her ears. It was almost as if she were deliberately proclaiming herself of importance.

First she curtsied to the Tzar, kissed his hand, and then his cheek, before she greeted the Prince.

"It is delightful to see you again, Ivan," she said, holding out her hand, "and I am so happy that you were able to get here so quickly."

The way she spoke made Prince Ivan look at her questioningly. Then the Tzar said:

"Eudoxia, who as well as being a Romanov, is also my God-daughter, has told me how much you two mean to each other."

As Vida, listening, drew in her breath, the Prince stiffened and the Tzar continued.

"I therefore, with much pleasure, give my consent and unqualified approval to your marriage!"

He spoke in a way which sounded sincere. As he did so, for one second the Princess's eyes met Vida's and she knew that this was the way in which she had very effectively taken her revenge.

After the Tzar had spoken there was silence until the Prince of Kiev said:

"My dear fellow, I had no idea that this was intended! My congratulations and of course my very best wishes to you both!"

He turned to the Tzar and added:

"You have certainly contrived, Your Majesty, to join together two of the most remarkably handsome people who ever existed! At their wedding it will be difficult to know who the congregation will admire the more—the bride or the bridegroom!"

He laughed at his own joke, and the Tzar laughed too.

Then with an unmistakably spiteful look in her eyes the Princess Eudoxia moved towards Vida and held out her hand.

As Vida curtsied Eudoxia said:

"I am sure, Countess, that you will offer me your good wishes. It is so nice to see you again after meeting you at dear Ivan's Castle."

Vida knew then who had planned this whole scene and had to admit it had been very cleverly thought out.

Furious because the Prince had been so engrossed with Vida at the Castle, the Princess must have left immediately, and having found the Tzar, asked for his permission for them to be married.

Yet for the Princess, womanlike, that had not been enough.

She was determined in addition to gloat over Vida personally, assuming her to be the Prince's newest interest. And doubtless, his mistress.

Forcing herself to smile, even while she felt as if a thousand knives were being driven into her heart, Vida said:

"It is true, Your Highness, that you will be the most beautiful bride Russia, or any other country for that matter, has ever seen and . . . of course I wish you the greatest happiness . . . now and for . . . ever!"

She could not control a little tremor in her voice as she said the last words.

But the Princess only gave her the triumphant smile of a woman who has got her revenge and turned what had seemed to be a defeat into a victory.

Prince Ivan had not yet spoken, and as if he sensed that something was wrong, the Tzar said somewhat heavily:

"I have always been fond of you, dear boy, and it is time you settled down and had a family. I was already married by the time I was your age."

Still the Prince did not speak, and the Tzar went on.

"You will of course be married in St. Petersburg, and hold your reception at the Winter Palace."

"That is extremely generous of Your Majesty," the Prince said at last.

Vida thought his voice to anybody except herself would have sounded calm and normal.

Only she was aware with her "sixth sense," of which they had talked together, that he was angry, almost uncontrollably angry at being tricked.

But he knew, as she did, that there was nothing he could do about it.

The Emperor of all the Russias had issued a decree, and there was nothing the Prince could do but obey.

Only when Vida had gone up to her room where Margit was waiting for her did she allow the smile she felt was fixed on her face as if it were glued there to fade.

As soon as the Housekeeper had escorted her into her bedroom and had shut the door behind her, her whole body seemed to sag as if the life in it were ebbing away from her.

As she moved forward, almost groping her way, to sit down on a *chaise longue* which stood at the foot of the bed, Margit gave a cry of concern.

"What's happened, Miss Vida? Are you ill?"

It was impossible for Vida to reply, and Margit said again:

"If you feel faint, I will get you some brandy."

"No, no, I am . . . all right," Vida managed to say.

She pulled her bonnet from her head and put it down beside her, then said in a voice that did not sound like her own:

"The Tzar has just . . . arranged that the . . . Prince shall . . . marry the Princess Eudoxia!"

Margit stared at her for a moment as if she had not understood. Then as she picked up Vida's bonnet she remarked:

"That's certainly a surprise, but there's no reason why it should concern you."

"Of course it concerns me!" Vida said. "He has no wish to . . . marry her!"

"Then he should not have played about with the

girl," Margit retorted. "I heard when we were in the Castle that one of the Prince's lady-guests had left in a precipitate way the morning after we arrived. The Housekeeper kept saying how strange it was when she had come intending to stay for at least a week! And her chaperone, who I believe was also her Lady-in-Waiting, had to leave too and was very cross about it!"

"The Princess was jealous because the Prince was paying too much attention to me!" Vida said.

"Well, it's no use crying over spilt milk," Margit said, "and if you ask me, the sooner we get away from here and back to normality, the better!"

"I agree with you," Vida replied. "The Princess obviously asked for me to accompany Prince Ivan here simply so that she could gloat over me."

"You can't trust these Russians!" Margit exclaimed.

They were talking in English and Vida suddenly was frightened in case anybody listening to the way Margit spoke would suspect that she was not Russian.

She put her fingers to her lips to warn Margit she was being indiscreet, and the old maid, taking the hint, said in French:

"I shouldn't say rude things about your country-women, should I, M'Lady? But I hope you haven't forgotten that you promised to stay with your relatives in Hungary as soon as we can get back."

"I have not forgotten," Vida said, "and all I want is to see my friends again."

She was, of course, thinking of her father and that when she told him the whole story he would understand and would not find fault with her.

Then as she thought of him and his warning, she told herself that if she had any pride at all she would not let the Princess, or for that matter, Prince Ivan, realise what she was feeling.

In any case, it was absurd that she should have believed all that he had said to her on the train, because even then there had been no future for them together.

She was quite certain that the idea of marriage had never crossed his mind, and just as he had tried to make love to her before in the Castle she suspected that when they returned there he would have attempted once again to make her his.

'It would have been very difficult to withstand him,' she thought, and then was ashamed that she should be so weak as to contemplate for one moment forsaking the principles that had been hers since she was a young girl.

She had been taught that it would be wrong to allow a man to kiss her unless she was to marry him.

Yet when the Prince had kissed her and brought her a rapture that was different from anything she had ever imagined in her dreams, it had not seemed wrong, but so right and so perfect that it had been divine.

"How can I question anything that seemed to come from God?" she asked herself now.

Yet she knew she was now being punished for what she had done, and there was no point in complaining about it.

She put her feet up on the *chaise longue,* lay back against the cushions, and shut her eyes.

Without realising it, she was calling on the Power that had sustained both her father and herself ever since she had worked with him.

When they had found themselves in difficult situations in which she had thought it would be absolutely impossible for him to extricate them without his identity being discovered, they had used the Power.

But what had happened in Russia was far more dangerous, far more frightening, than anything she had ever experienced before.

It was stupid to pretend that if the Secret Police had actually caught him as they intended he would not have been tortured until he divulged the information they required.

After which he would certainly have been exterminated.

But he was safe, and the price she had to pay for his safety was that she was hopelessly in love with a man who had attracted dozens of women before her and would doubtless attract dozens more in the future.

Now he was being compelled to pay the penalty, not for a criminal offence, but for his philandering.

The Princess Eudoxia had turned the tables on him, and in such a clever way that he was now a prisoner for the rest of his life.

Vida knew enough about Russia to be aware that not only was the Tzar's word law, but also that anybody who offended him in the slightest degree could find themselves on the gallows, or at the very least being sent to Siberia.

She had heard so many tales of the terrible sufferings of even noblemen who had upset the Tzar in one way or another.

They were marched off in chains to the salt mines, their possessions confiscated, their families left to starve.

There was no question of that happening to Prince Ivan.

He would marry the beautiful Princess Eudoxia and become through her even closer to the Tzar than he was already.

As far as she herself was concerned, Vida was certain he had always been a man who was out of reach, and he would be crying for himself and his freedom which had meant so much to him.

There would always be other women in his life, but she was sure that Princess Eudoxia would be possessive, and very jealous.

He would not be able to flaunt his love-affairs openly as he had been able to do until now.

"I suppose it is poetic justice," Vida said to herself.

But that thought did not help to cure the ache in her heart that was like a physical wound, or the feeling that an icy hand, when she least expected it, had clutched her round the neck, choking the very breath out of her body.

By the time she had had a bath and changed into one of the exotic gowns she had brought to wear at the Castle, she told herself that she was British and must not appear overwhelmed or even disconcerted by what had occurred.

Yet because she really felt ill, she made Margit give her a spoonful of brandy which they always carried for medicinal reasons when they were travelling.

When she had done so, she thought her eyes looked brighter and less stricken.

She applied a little rouge to her cheeks, darkened her eye-lashes with mascara, and wearing a tiara which had belonged to her mother and which she thought would compare favourably with any of the Princess Eudoxia's jewels, she slowly descended the staircase.

A flunkey was waiting in the large hall to lead her to the room where everybody was to meet before dinner.

As she entered it, Vida was glad to see it was quite a large party.

Some of the guests, she had learnt from Margit, were staying in the house; others had been invited to meet the Tzar.

The men looked resplendent, wearing their decorations on their evening-coats or uniforms.

But the Prince stood out, wearing the ribbon of St. Michael across his chest, and innumerable diamond decorations on his evening-coat.

The women glittered like Christmas trees, but Vida knew she could hold her own amongst them.

When her host introduced her, she took pains to make herself pleasant, paying the women compliments and smiling invitingly at the men.

Everybody was chattering gaily until as they lined up formally before the Tzar entered the room, a sudden hush fell like fog over the assembled company.

It was then that Vida realised that standing opposite her was the Prince.

For a moment their eyes met, and she thought there was an expression of pain in his.

Then as she looked away she told herself that she was not concerned with his feelings, but her own.

What she had to do, as quickly as was humanly possible, was to forget him.

At the same time, without really meaning to, she glanced at him again.

He was looking at her and now, despite herself, she felt that little flicker of excitement within her that always came a second before he took her in his arms.

Then as she tried to prevent it flooding through her heart and up to her lips, the Princess Eudoxia moved across the room from where she had been standing and slipped her arm through Prince Ivan's.

As she did so she threw back her head and looked up at him, the long line of her neck very lovely and very sensuous against the dark texture of his coat.

Her lips were slightly parted, her eyes very eloquent, as if she told him aloud how much she wanted him.

It was then, instead of ecstasy, that Vida felt there was murder in her heart, and she was frightened by the violence of her own feelings.

chapter seven

HAVING cried herself to sleep, Vida awoke feeling miserable with an aching head.

She lay in the dim light wishing she need not rouse herself, wanting to drift back into unconsciousness.

She knew that with every breath she drew the pain she was feeling became harder to bear, and although she tried to tell herself it was ridiculous she felt that she was being crucified.

Margit came into the room to pull back the curtains.

"It's time you were up, Miss Vida," she said, "as I understand we're leaving today."

Vida forced herself to open her eyes.

Last night, after what she thought to anyone would have been an extremely dull evening compared to those she had enjoyed at the Castle, the Tzar had retired soon after midnight, and the party broke up.

Vida had learnt that His Imperial Majesty disliked

late hours, and when he was at the Winter Palace he would wander awkwardly through the Reception Rooms until at two o'clock he would begin to look at his watch.

"Most Russian parties," her father had explained, "do not end until breakfast-time at six o'clock in the morning, but the Tzar has a disconcerting habit of dismissing the orchestra one by one. When the band is reduced to a piano player and a violinist, even the most ardent party-goer knows it is time to go home!"

Vida had laughed at the time, but she was therefore not surprised at the Tzar's behaviour last night, although on this occasion he was not the host.

He had talked first to one person, then to another, hardly finishing one conversation before he started the next.

She had, in fact, had a short talk with him soon after they came from the Dining-Room.

"I cannot remember ever meeting anybody of your name before, Countess," he said abruptly, almost as if he were accusing her of deceiving him.

"I am afraid, Your Majesty, that most of my relatives are dead," Vida replied. "Those who are left are, I understand, very old, and seldom travel far from their homes."

He was appraising her almost as if she were a horse and he was sizing up her points. Then he said:

"I understand you are a widow. I presume you are looking for another husband."

Vida managed to answer in a soft voice:

"I hope, one day, Your Majesty, that I shall find somebody I can love and who will love me."

"Love?" the Tzar exclaimed sharply. "What you

want, you foolish woman, is security and a man who can protect you."

"I hope I may be lucky enough to find one, Sire," Vida answered.

He walked away from her as if he thought any further conversation was a waste of time.

Making desperate efforts not to look towards the Prince, Vida talked to an elderly woman who was seated on a nearby sofa.

When the guests who had come from outside the Palace started to leave, she saw the Prince standing alone at the end of the room and wondered if she dared go to his side.

As if because she was thinking of him he became aware of her, he turned to look at her and for a moment their eyes met.

Then before she could tell what he was feeling or thinking, he looked away and deliberately walked to the side of Princess Eudoxia, who was saying farewell to one of the departing guests.

To Vida it was as if he told her pointedly that he had no further use for her, and for a moment she felt the room swim round her and everything go blank.

Then her pride made her force away the faintness that was beginning to seep over her and picking up a glass which she saw on a side-table, she drank from it.

She had no idea if it contained water or wine, or even poison for that matter.

While she felt some of the weakness fade, she was aware it would be wise for her to go to her bedroom.

She passed one or two people who were saying good night to their host at the door.

Then just as she reached the Prince of Kiev and was about to make her excuses for retiring early the Princess Eudoxia walked towards her.

"I understand, Countess," she said, "that you are leaving tomorrow, and so of course I must say farewell."

Vida curtsied.

"Goodbye, Your Highness."

"I hope it really is goodbye," the Princess said in a low voice that only she could hear. "I shall make every effort, Countess, to see that we do not meet again."

There was venom in her voice and in the expression of her eyes, and Vida did not reply.

She merely curtsied a little deeper than she had before, hoping the Princess was aware she was being deliberately sarcastic in doing so, then said good night to her host.

When she reached her bedroom she felt as if the ceiling had crashed down on her head and the whole future was dark.

Only as she started to undress did the tears come running down her cheeks, and she felt as if each one of them were a drop of blood from her heart.

Now, surprised by what Margit had said, Vida asked:

"Who told you we were leaving today?"

"I was told so by one of the Palace servants," Margit replied. "He said that a carriage would be waiting to take us to the railway station at one o'clock."

Vida did not answer and Margit went on.

"The servant informed me there would be luncheon

arranged for us here at noon, but as we are travelling in His Highness's train there will be plenty to eat, and very much better food than in this place!"

Vida's eyes were wide as she asked:

"How do you know we are travelling in His Highness's train?"

"His valet told me," Margit answered.

"Did he say anything else?"

"Yes, he said that the Tzar with the Prince and Princess Eudoxia were being shown round the Monastery of the Caves, and would not be back for luncheon."

Vida knew that the Monastery of the Caves was one of the sights of Kiev, and all the Princes of Kiev were buried in the very ancient church belonging to the monastery.

When she read about it she had thought it was something she would like to see, but there was now no hope of that.

At the same time, she was grateful to the Prince, even if he was no longer interested in her, for making sure that her exit from Russia would be in comfort.

It was an agony to remember how happy she had been with him when they had travelled together in his train to Kiev.

She remembered he had said there were other things he wanted to say to her on the return journey.

But now she was returning alone, while he would be in Kiev, and after that in St. Petersburg with his beautiful bride-to-be.

'He is just a meteor flashing through my life as Papa said he would be,' Vida thought, 'and I was very foolish to think that a meteor could stop long enough . . . even for me to tell him that . . . I love him.'

She felt the tears come again into her eyes and lay back against the pillows.

Because she was so silent, Margit was a little worried and went to the side of the bed.

"Now, what are you upsetting yourself about, Miss Vida?" she asked. "If it's His Highness, just forget him!"

Vida merely shut her eyes and made no reply.

"His valet tells me," Margit went on, "that Princess Eudoxia has been determined to marry him for the last year, 'chasing him as if he were a wild stag' was how he put it."

"I do not wish to hear about it," Vida murmured.

"All right, have it your own way," Margit said. "But as you well know, no nobleman of any importance in this country can marry without the Tzar's permission, and if on the other hand His Majesty says they're to marry, there's no question of anyone saying no."

"I am aware of . . . that."

She felt as she spoke that her voice was coming from a long distance away.

A little later she got out of bed, and after she had had a bath she felt a little better.

She washed her face, then put on the cosmetics she used as the Countess Kărólzi, thinking that it was for the last time.

She did not put on the spectacular travelling-gown she had worn to arrive in, but wore instead one of her own pretty gowns which had a light coat to go over it, and a bonnet trimmed with flowers rather than feathers.

"You look strange in those clothes with your face painted like an actress!" Margit remarked.

"I know," Vida said. "As soon as we get on the train I shall wash it off and be myself. I am sick of deception and lies and being afraid to speak."

"So am I," Margit agreed. "The best thing we can do, Miss Vida, is to go straight back to England and make the master behave himself."

Vida laughed.

"We should have to work very hard to do that! Do not forget, Margit, he is to be our Ambassador in Paris, so that we shall be in a very gay city and doubtless one full of intrigues."

Margit sniffed.

At the same time Vida knew she was thinking that France was a very different place from Russia, and at least they would not be afraid every moment of encountering the Secret Police.

Thinking there was no point in going downstairs if everybody staying in the house was out to luncheon, Margit had the food brought to the boudoir next to her bedroom.

It was quite appetising, but Vida felt as if every mouthful would choke her. Only out of politeness did she help herself to a little of what the footmen offered her, and took a few sips of wine.

When it was time to go she walked down the stairs followed by Margit, and found as she expected a closed carriage waiting for them.

One of the Prince's Aides-de-Camps saw her off, and she asked him to thank His Highness for his hospitality and say how much she had enjoyed herself.

Then she and Margit drove away, and they had

hardly spoken a word before they reached the railway station.

Vida knew when they saw the Prince's magnificent white and red train waiting for them that Margit was delighted to travel in such style.

The ordinary trains in Russia, unless there was a special coach attached for them, were reputedly uncomfortable and often dirty.

Henri was waiting on the platform with some Palace officials and there were, of course, the usual number of Prince Ivan's servants wearing his livery.

There was everything to make Vida comfortable, and as soon as she sat down in the Drawing-Room Car she was offered champagne and caviar, both of which she refused.

It seemed a long time before they started, and Henri explained that as the Prince's train was unscheduled, they had to wait for the line to be clear before they could leave.

When at last the engine puffed slowly out of the station, the servants from the Palace bowing as they left, Vida went to the bedroom she had used before to remove her bonnet.

As she told Margit she would do, she washed her face, feeling, as she did so, that she was washing away the last evidence of the wild adventure which had brought her to Russia to try to save her father's life.

She had succeeded; of course she had succeeded, but at the cost of losing her heart and loving a man who she knew had spoilt her for every other man in the world.

'I suppose now I shall never marry,' she thought wistfully.

The train gathered speed and with every throb of the wheels she thought her heart was saying goodbye to the Prince.

She must have looked very pale and drawn, for Margit insisted that she should lie down on the bed and rest.

"There's nothing for you to do but look out of the window," she said, "and the landscape isn't any different from how it looked when we came here yesterday."

"Was it only yesterday?" Vida murmured.

She was thinking that centuries might have passed since she had sat in the Drawing-Room Car and felt herself thrill at everything the Prince said to her, and known a wild excitement from the touch of his hand.

"I will lie down, Margit," she said hastily, thinking perhaps she would sleep and that way have some peace.

She took off her slippers and lay down on the bed.

But it was impossible to sleep, and she found herself seeing with closed eyes the Prince's face and hearing his voice.

She thought over every word he had ever said to her.

Then she felt his lips against hers and wondered wildly why she had been so foolish as to send him away from her bedroom when he had wanted to make love to her.

'At least I would have had that to remember,' she thought now.

Then she was ashamed of forgetting her principles, her mother's teaching, and her belief in what was right and wrong.

"It is over! It is over!" she could hear the wheels

saying, as if they must keep repeating the words to impress them on her memory.

* * *

Vida must have dozed for a while, for she was awoken by Margit standing beside the bed saying that the servants wondered if she was ready for dinner.

"Is it really as late as that, Margit?" Vida asked.

"It's getting on," Margit said, "and if you'll take my advice, you'll have something to eat and then let me put you to bed. We've a long way to go, so the stewards tell me."

Vida wanted to ask to which town in Hungary they were going.

She knew that the Russian trains did not go to Sarospatak. Otherwise she would have taken a train to the Prince's Castle rather than travel by carriage.

It was too much trouble to work it out, and she merely agreed to what Margit advised and went into the Drawing-Room Car.

The Prince's servants brought her what she knew was a delicious dinner.

But again she was not hungry, although rather than disappoint the Chef, who she was sure had made a great effort on her behalf, she tried to eat a little of everything she was offered.

Darkness came swiftly and the curtains were pulled over the windows, so that she could no longer see whether they were still in wooded country, or passing over the flat, fertile ground which the Prince had pointed out to her on their way to Kiev.

But she was not really interested, and when Margit

helped her to undress, without thinking she put on one of her pretty nightgowns and her negligee and sat down beside the bed.

"Now, go to sleep, Miss Vida," Margit said. "I'm going to my own carriage and, if you're not tired, I am!"

"You look tired," Vida said, "so do not worry about me. Think about yourself for a change."

"I'll do that when we're safely over the border!" Margit retorted.

Strangely enough, when Margit had left her, Vida did not get into bed.

Instead, she went back into the Drawing-Room Car and sat down on the sofa.

It was where she had sat with the Prince, and she felt almost as if he were there beside her and she could tell him what she was feeling.

Once again she was thinking back over the things he had said to her, the feelings he had evoked in her, and it was some time later that she realised that the train had come to a standstill.

She supposed that once again they were waiting until the line was clear, or perhaps a train travelling towards Kiev had to pass them first.

But when the train had stopped she no longer felt haunted by the sound of the wheels.

The lights in the car had been dimmed before the servants left, but it was still easy to see how tastefully it was furnished and how luxurious it was.

'It is part of the perfection he is always seeking,' Vida thought with a faint smile.

It was at that moment that she heard the sound of horses galloping and thought it was strange that anybody should be in such a hurry.

The sound came nearer, then stopped abruptly outside her carriage.

It was then with a sense of fear that she wondered if it was the Secret Police who had just arrived.

Could the Princess Eudoxia, in her jealousy of her, have perhaps discovered in some way that she was not who she appeared to be?

Had the Secret Police decided that she should be subjected to one of their interrogations?

The terror of it struck through Vida like a flaming sword.

She heard voices, but she could not move. Anyway, if she wished to hide, there was nowhere she could go, and she clasped her hands together until the knuckles showed white.

Then she heard the outer door of the Drawing-Room Car open and footsteps in the passage which led to the inner door.

Somebody came into the car and for a moment she dared not look; she dared not even breathe.

Then as if she were forced to turn her head she looked round.

Standing looking at her was the Prince!

For a second Vida thought she must be dreaming. Then as he came towards her she gave a little cry that seemed to be strangled in her throat.

He drew nearer still, and now, as if she suddenly came alive, Vida rose to her feet.

"You are . . . here!" she managed to say in a voice that did not sound like her own. "B-but . . . why have you . . . come . . . ? Is something . . . wrong?"

As she spoke, it flashed through her mind that perhaps he had come to tell her that her father had been arrested.

But he was smiling as he put his arms around her and drew her close against him.

"I have come, my darling, for you!" he said, and his lips came down on hers.

Vida did not understand, but as he kissed her, streaks of lightning flashed through her body.

A wild, irresistible ecstasy seemed to rise like a flame which burnt against the fire on the Prince's lips.

He kissed her until she felt as if her whole being merged into him, and she was no longer herself, but his, and they were one.

Then as she felt the train begin to move and the wheels turn over on the rails beneath them, the Prince drew her down onto the sofa, still holding her closely in his arms.

Only when he was kissing the softness of her neck as he had done before, did she ask:

"Why . . . are you here? Oh . . . Ivan . . . what has happened?"

"My darling, my sweet!" he said. "My heart, my life! Did you really think I could lose you?"

"What . . . are you . . . saying?"

"I am saying, my precious, that I am endangering your life and mine in a mad gamble, and we must start praying that we will not be caught."

Vida put her hands flat on his chest, pushing him a little away from her.

"Tell me . . . explain to me . . . what you are saying," she begged. "I . . . I cannot understand."

He smiled at her before he said:

"There is only one thing to understand, which is that I love you!"

"And I love you," Vida replied, "but . . . I thought I should . . . never see you . . . again."

"I knew you were thinking that, my precious little love, but there was no way I could ask you to trust me."

He would have kissed her again, but Vida said:

"I still do not . . . understand."

The Prince pulled her close to him and said:

"We are running away, my lovely one, and as I have already said, we must pray that we will reach the frontier without being apprehended."

"You mean . . . you are coming with . . . me?" Vida stammered.

"I mean that I am going to marry you the moment we are out of Russia."

Vida drew in her breath and stared at him as if she thought she could not have heard him aright.

"M-marry me?"

"You made it very clear that you would not accept my love any other way," the Prince said with a hint of laughter in his voice.

"But . . . you are to marry the . . . Princess Eudoxia!"

"That was her idea, not mine."

"But . . . the Tzar . . . ?"

"The Tzar will be very angry," the Prince replied, "very angry indeed! However, once we are out of the country there is nothing he can do about it."

Vida stared at him in bewilderment.

"But still . . . I do not understand. Surely he will confiscate . . . your Castle, your estate . . . ?"

"He is welcome to them!" the Prince said. "The only thing I want, my beautiful soul of my soul, is you!"

"You . . . cannot be . . . serious!"

"I am very serious," the Prince answered.

Vida felt the tears come into her eyes.

"How can you do anything so wonderful...so marvellous?" she asked brokenly. "At the same time I cannot let you...do this for me."

"I think you will find it very hard to stop me."

"I love you. You know that I love you," Vida said. "But suppose you regret giving up all your...possessions...your wealth?"

The Prince looked at her for a long moment. Then he said:

"Are you afraid of being poor with me?"

"No...of course not!" Vida replied. "I love you so overwhelmingly that if we had to live in a tent on the Hungarian steppes, or in a little cottage in England, I would be supremely...blissfully...happy to share it with...you."

She spoke with a passionate note of sincerity in her voice which brought a look of tenderness to the Prince's eyes that few people had ever seen.

"I believe you really mean that!" he said slowly.

"You know I mean it! But you have never been poor, and although Papa may spare me a little money, you would have to give up so many luxuries that I cannot believe that...any woman would be...worth it."

"*Any* woman would *not* be worth it! The only thing I am not giving up is *you*. You are different, my darling, and it is going to take me a lifetime to tell you how different you are."

"That is what I want you to say," Vida said, "but I still think you do not...understand."

"What do I not understand?"

"That if we live like ordinary people you will not

165

be important as you are now and you will not be able to enjoy the ... perfection which you are ... always seeking."

She gave a little cry, and then said:

"I have to make you ... think of this before you do anything ... irrevocable, something you may ... later regret."

She moved a little way from the Prince and said, not looking at him:

"Have you thought of what ... life would be like without so many ... servants ... without your outstandingly beautiful horses ... without your private train?"

She drew in her breath before she went on.

"You have always been able to entertain your friends in unsurpassed luxury, travel wherever you want to go, and do a million things which I told you once made you ... seem like a ... genie."

Her voice dropped a little lower before she asked:

"Can you ... really be sure ... that I am ... worth all that?"

The Prince reached out his hand to turn her face towards him and said:

"Look at me, Vida! Look into my eyes!"

She thrilled at his touch and obeyed him.

As her eyes met his she could feel their vibrations joining in that inexplicable and magnetic way that they had joined before.

It told her that whatever happened she would never find another man to take his place.

"I love you," the Prince said in his deep voice, "and you love me! Do you think anything in the world could matter beside what we feel for each other?"

"Not . . . where I am . . . concerned," Vida whispered.

He did not speak, but merely pulled her roughly against him, and now he was kissing her with a fire that seemed to burn through her whole body.

It was like diving into the heart of the sun.

He kissed her until she felt that even if she died at this moment she would have touched perfection, and nothing could ever be so wonderful again.

Only when they were both breathless did the Prince say:

"Do not argue with me any longer! I have no intention of listening! I know what I want, I know what I intend to have, and that is you!"

"I love you . . . I love you!"

He kissed her and then with his arms around her he said:

"Say that again and again. It is all I want to hear."

For a moment Vida just shut her eyes because she felt moved by the glory of their love. Then she asked:

"Tell me . . . exactly how you . . . got away and what is . . . happening."

"I only want to kiss you and go on kissing you," the Prince replied, "but I understand you are curious."

"Very curious!" Vida whispered. "I still find it hard to believe that you are . . . really . . . here."

"I am here! I am not a genie and I am real!"

His lips moved over the softness of her cheeks before he said:

"After we are married, my darling, I will prove to you how real I am so that you will never doubt it again."

He kissed her straight little nose, each corner of

her mouth, then when he would have kissed her lips she put up her hand to prevent him.

"I am still . . . curious."

Even as she spoke he felt her quiver against him and smiled.

"You are trying to prevent me from doing what I want to do, which is to kiss you."

Then, as if he thought he had teased her enough, he said:

"When the Tzar told me I was to marry Eudoxia I realised she had set a trap for me, and I was extremely angry!"

"I knew . . . that."

"She has wanted to marry me for quite a time," the Prince went on, "but very stupidly I did not take her seriously."

"You mean . . . so many women have wanted the same thing that you . . . thought it was . . . unimportant!"

"I did not intend to marry anybody," the Prince replied, "until I met you."

"Oh, Ivan, did you . . . really want to marry me?"

"I knew from the very first moment I saw you that you were different from anybody I had ever met before, and that you attracted me almost unbearably."

He smiled down at her and went on.

"If I had known you were your father's daughter, I think I would have asked you to marry me on the first night you came to the Castle!"

"But instead . . . you suggested something . . . very different!"

"That was your fault, pretending to be a widow and an experienced woman, even though my instinct told me otherwise. That made me think I could make you mine, and still remain free."

"But . . . why do you not want . . . that now?"

"Because you are my Dream-Come-True, the woman I have always wanted as my own, the woman to whom, strange though it may seem, I shall be faithful for the rest of my life."

The way he spoke made Vida feel as if he were enveloped by the Divine Light she had seen around him before.

All she could do was to make a sound of utter happiness and put her head against his shoulder.

"When you closed the gates of Paradise against me," the Prince said, "I knew I could never lose you."

"So after I had . . . gone away you . . . followed me."

"I followed you, and I also wanted to rescue your father. Apart from adoring you and worshipping the ground you stand on, I am also very proud, very proud indeed, to marry the daughter of a man I admire more than any other man I have ever known."

Vida felt the tears come into her eyes.

"How can you say anything so . . . marvellous," she asked, "and which makes me so . . . happy?"

The Prince kissed her forehead before he said:

"I feel I have fought a million battles for you. I can never begin to describe what I felt when the Tzar announced his permission and approval for my marriage to Eudoxia."

"You did not think it was . . . something you . . . should do?"

"I knew it was something I had no intention of doing," the Prince answered sharply. "But, my precious, my only chance of escaping and, incidentally, yours, was for me to pretend to agree and to make myself pleasant to Eudoxia. As you must realise, as a Romanov, she can be very vindictive and also very dangerous."

Vida gave a little shiver.

"Do you mean . . . she might injure . . . me?"

"If she thought there was any likelihood of my being here at this moment," the Prince said in a hard voice, "she would undoubtedly have you killed, and I should be on my way to Siberia!"

Vida gave a cry of horror.

"Suppose . . . suppose that . . . happens to you . . . now?"

"That is what we have to avoid," the Prince said in a quiet voice.

"Tell me . . . tell me . . . exactly what you have planned."

Vida knew as she spoke that once again she was almost frantic with terror, not for herself, but for the Prince.

For the moment she could think only of him, of him dying in the salt mines or being tortured by the Tzar's Secret Police.

It made her feel that to give him up when she loved him so much was a sacrifice she must make, whatever the cost to her.

"I . . . I cannot . . . allow you to do this!" she said.

"It is too late now to stop me," the Prince replied. "As you must have guessed, my precious, while the train carried you away from the station at Kiev so that the Palace officials were able to tell Eudoxia you had left, you were actually only five miles outside the city."

"Then you rode here," Vida said, following what he was saying. "Did no one see you leave the Palace?"

"My men were waiting for me as I had arranged, and they had told the grooms in the stables that they had been ordered by me to go on special night manoeuvres to test themselves and their horses in the dark."

Vida was listening intently as he went on.

"When I joined them, enveloped in a military cloak, I looked just like them, and the grooms had no idea I was not an ordinary soldier."

"Then you came to me here."

"I had given my orders where the train was to wait. It is an isolated place where it is very unlikely anybody will report its presence."

Vida gave a sigh.

"You make it sound so easy," she said, "but what happens . . . now?"

"Now we are making for Cernauti," he said, "which is the nearest foreign frontier town to Kiev."

"That is in Rumania."

"What does it matter where it is so long as it is out of Russia?" the Prince asked. "Unless we are delayed, we should cross the frontier tomorrow about noon, and I reckon we have a start of at least seven or eight hours before anybody realises I am not asleep in the Palace."

"Oh, darling," Vida cried, "I am praying that yet another of your plans will work out perfectly, and this time it is rather more important than any of the others."

"Very much more important!" the Prince agreed.

"When we reach Rumania, where are we going?"

"I will tell you a little later how we are to cross

the frontier," he said, "and after that we are going to another of my Castles, which I hope you will appreciate. It is in the centre of Hungary, and is where my horses come from."

Vida looked up at him and exclaimed:

"I had forgotten you had other houses! I remember now you have a Villa in Monte Carlo."

"I have a Castle in Hungary," the Prince said, "which is, or will be, in many ways as beautiful as the one I am leaving behind in Russia."

He knew what she was feeling without her saying so, and he said gently:

"Does it make you happier to know that I am not going to be as poverty-stricken as you thought?"

"Very . . . very . . . happy!"

"I will let you into a secret. I have been expecting something like this to happen for some time."

"You have?"

"Not that I should marry anybody as wonderful, as beautiful, as perfect as you are, my angel, but there was always the chance that in the course of my various activities with your father and other people like him, I should be caught out and discovered."

He paused and Vida asked:

"What did you do?"

"The moment the Tzar told me I was to marry Eudoxia," the Prince replied, "I sent a message to put into operation the removal, as I had planned it, of my treasures from the Castle."

Vida looked at him wide-eyed as he went on.

"Vans have been travelling all day, taking them over the border into Hungary."

"I do not . . . believe it!"

"It is true," the Prince smiled. "Of course not

everything will be saved, but I hope to have got away the most valuable of my pictures, my icons, ivories, porcelain, and the gold plates and goblets which have been in my family for generations."

Vida gave a cry of excitement.

"It is so like you and I am glad, so very . . . very glad! I shall . . . not feel so . . . guilty for allowing you to . . . elope with me."

"I do not feel in the least guilty," the Prince said. "I think, my precious, it is a very exciting way to start our life together, and something we shall always remember."

"I shall always . . . remember what you have . . . given up for me," Vida said softly.

She felt the Prince did not understand, and went on.

"You are Russian and are giving up your country which you love, and your position at Court which I well know to every Russian is of great importance."

"It is of course very important," the Prince agreed, "except for one thing."

"What is that?"

"Love is more important than anything else: the love which all Russians seek in their souls, but so seldom find."

He spoke very solemnly as he said:

"My love for you is totally different from what I have felt for any other woman, and as you are aware, there have been many of them. I have enjoyed them, they have attracted me, charmed my eyes, my mind, and sometimes my heart. But not one of them, and this is the truth, my lovely Vida, has touched my soul."

He gave a very soft laugh as he said:

"I began to think that such a thing was impossible, and that I would never find the woman whose love would make me feel as if she were enveloped with the light of the Divine, because she came from God."

Vida knew this was what she had felt about him.

What he said made her so happy that she could only stretch out her arms and pull his head down to hers.

Once again he kissed her and carried her up towards the stars. Then they talked until dawn came.

After that the Prince insisted that Vida go to bed and rest.

"We have things to do later in the day," he said, "for which we must have all our wits about us, and therefore you must rest, my precious."

"I do not want . . . to leave you," Vida whispered.

"Once we are married, as I intend we shall be by tomorrow evening," the Prince replied, "or at the very latest the following day, then you will never leave me for one moment. Go to sleep for a few hours, my darling, and dream of me, as I shall be dreaming of you."

He drew her into the bedroom and waited while she got into bed, then he tucked her in and kissed her very gently on the lips.

"I love you! I adore you! I worship you!" he said. "Now and for all eternity!"

* * *

Vida was awoken by Margit bringing her a cup of coffee and saying:

"His Highness is waiting for you in the Drawing-Room Car."

"Why did you not tell me sooner?" Vida asked. "I might have been with him!"

"He's been asleep, just as you have, Miss Vida," Margit replied.

Suddenly there were tears in her eyes.

"Oh, Miss Vida, His Highness says you're to be married, and I don't know if I'm on my head or my heels!"

"Yes . . . we are to be married," Vida said, "and I am happy, Margit, so very, very happy."

"I never thought it'd happen, not in a million years! But he's everything a woman could want in a man, and there's no denying that."

"No, Margit, and I shall not attempt to deny it!" Vida laughed.

She got out of bed and washed, then as she looked for her clothes, Margit brought her a peasant dress.

She looked at it in astonishment and Margit explained:

"His Highness said you are to put this on, and I'm to do your hair in two plaits as if you were a young girl of about sixteen."

"I . . . I do not understand."

"I expect His Highness will tell you his plan," Margit said, "but remember, we all have to get across the frontier."

Vida suddenly felt afraid again.

They might be prevented from leaving Russia, at least held in custody until instructions arrived from the Tzar's Secret Police.

She put on the peasant clothes, which were not new. They had been patched in places, and the blouse had been skillfully darned where there were tears on the sleeves.

There was a woollen shawl to go round her shoulders, and that had been washed a number of times.

There were rough shoes for her feet and socks instead of stockings for her legs.

She felt a little shy and very unlike herself as she went into the Drawing-Room Car, where the Prince was waiting.

He smiled at her appearance and as he rose Vida ran towards him to say:

"What is this all about? Why do you want me to dress like this?"

He pulled her down on the sofa beside him. Then he said:

"We have made very good progress, my darling; in fact, I have never known my train to go so fast. But we have to be very careful, as you will understand."

"Of course," Vida said, "but what are we to do?"

"When we have had our luncheon," the Prince answered, "we shall arrive at a small station which is about five miles short of the border."

Vida listened as he went on.

"We are going to get out there, and we will wait for the ordinary afternoon train which goes to Cernauti. After we have passed into Rumania, my own train, which will be waiting in a siding, will follow us. If it is searched, as I expect it will be, there will be nobody on board except for the attendants."

"Do you think they will let it through?"

"I am sure they will," the Prince said. "They will have no excuse not to, for they will be told it has been sent to collect a number of my guests who are coming to stay with me at my Castle."

"It sounds a . . . very clever plan," Vida said, but there was a tremor in her voice.

She felt afterwards she had underestimated the Prince by being in the least nervous.

A quarter of a mile before the station of which he had spoken, which was situated in a wooded part of the country, the Prince's train came to a halt and there stepped out an elderly farmer—Henri, his wife—Margit, and their daughter, Vida.

They set off to walk towards the station, appearing a little tired after what had been an excursion into Russia to see some friends and relatives.

When they arrived on the platform there were a number of young Hungarian Hussars returning from Russia to their own country in a train which passed through the north of Rumania and from there into Hungary.

The Hussars were wearing somewhat worn uniforms, but the Officer in Charge looked very elegant with his coat, as was traditional in Hungarian uniform, hanging over one shoulder.

He also wore a curly black moustache and except that she vibrated towards him, Vida would have found it hard to recognise him as the Prince.

The soldiers were all laughing and talking and making jokes, and the few Russians in charge of the station took no notice of the farmer with his wife and daughter who sat down on a wooden seat to await the arrival of the train.

When it came in it was already filled with a miscellaneous collection of passengers—Ukrainians, Russians, and quite a number of Bulgarians.

The soldiers piled into the cheapest carriages, which

already seemed overcrowded.

The Officer travelled alone, and the farmer and his wife and daughter occupied the next carriage, which was slightly more expensive than the one in which the soldiers were travelling.

The train started off again and fifteen minutes later they were at the frontier.

There were a number of soldiers on the Russian side to inspect the papers of the travellers, but being mostly Ukrainians they looked at them in a perfunctory manner.

They were far more pleasant, Vida was sure, than the Russians would have been in the Balkan States.

At the same time, she felt tense and afraid until the papers Henri handed to the soldier were returned and he climbed out of the carriage, slamming the door behind him.

A few minutes later they were over the border.

The inspection in Rumania was very casual; in fact the soldier inspecting the travellers merely looked through the windows and never even asked for their papers.

As the engine gathered speed, Margit leaned back and said:

"Thank God! We are free, and I wouldn't go back even if somebody gave me a million pounds!"

Vida slipped her hand into the old maid's.

"You have been wonderful, Margit dear," she said, "and now all we have to do is to find Papa and live happily ever afterwards."

When a half hour later she joined the Prince on the station platform of a small town, she felt as if they were both enveloped by a rainbow.

They did not say very much. He stood beside her and ten minutes later the white and red train with his coat-of-arms emblazoned on it came puffing towards them.

When they had stepped into the Drawing-Room Car and the train had started off again, he pulled off his moustache, threw his Hussar's hat onto the floor, and took Vida in his arms.

Then he kissed her wildly, passionately, and with an intensity which told her, despite his outward confidence and calmness, he had been desperately afraid that at the last moment his plan might have gone wrong.

"We have ... won! We have ... won!" the Prince said. "The only thing that really matters, my precious, is that you are safe, and although it may not be possible for us to be married tonight, we will be married first thing tomorrow morning, when we reach my Castle."

"We must let Papa know where we are."

"I have already sent a telegram to tell him to join us," the Prince replied.

"You think of everything!"

"I think of you," he answered, "and as you want what I want, that is not very difficult."

He kissed her again.

They had a delicious dinner and when the table was cleared away they sat on the sofa. Vida put her head on the Prince's shoulder and said:

"How can all this have happened? If I had not defied the Marquess of Salisbury by going to Russia to find Papa, we would never have met."

"I think these things are ordained," the Prince said, "and, my beautiful one, we have been journeying towards each other since the beginning of time. To-morrow we will be one person, and nothing will ever separate us again."

"Are you . . . sure of that?" Vida asked. "Even now I am . . . afraid that at the last moment . . . something may . . . happen."

"It is too late for fears, doubts, or anything else except love."

He held her against him and said:

"I love you! God, how I love you! If you ever tried to run away from me again, I think I would kill you!"

She laughed up at him but she knew from the deep tone of his voice and the expression in his eyes that he meant what he said.

"I could never leave you," she said. "I will love you and look after you, and prevent you from going into danger . . . and of course . . . try to make you happy."

"That is all I want you to say. In the meantime, we will start a new life in Hungary, or if you prefer it we could go to France."

"I am not . . . interested in your . . . possessions."

"I am only boasting a little that I have them." The Prince laughed.

"They will come in useful when we have a family," Vida said. "One of your sons can have a Castle in Hungary, another a Chateau in France, and a third a house in England!"

The Prince laughed again. At the same time she saw a sudden fire in his eyes.

"What happens if we have four sons and some daughters?" he asked.

"The daughters will doubtless marry husbands who

are nearly as handsome as you," Vida answered, "and your fourth son can have the Villa in Monte Carlo, even though he may turn into a gambler!"

"That is what I am," the Prince said. "I gambled with everything I possessed, and I shall never forget, my precious, that you were prepared to be poor with me."

"I never . . . dreamt when I was so . . . miserable the night before I left Kiev that you would . . . come to join me," Vida said. "Oh, Ivan, darling, darling Ivan, how can I ever tell you how . . . much I love you, or how . . . happy I am?"

"Is there any need for words?"

The Prince's lips came down on hers as he spoke.

Then he was kissing her demandingly and with a fierceness that told her how frightened he had been that he might have lost her.

At the same time, there was now something different in his kisses which had not been there before.

The love she knew that he now gave her came from his soul as well as from his heart, for she was the perfect wife he had sought in his dreams.

She was the woman who would open for him the gates of Paradise and of Heaven itself.

God had watched over them, protected them, and brought them through every peril to safety and peace.

"I love . . . you," Vida murmured.

"I love you, heart of my heart, soul of my soul," the Prince replied. "You are mine—all mine!"

the world record and has continued for the following seven years with twenty-four, twenty, twenty-three, twenty-four, twenty-four, twenty-five, and twenty-three. She is in the *Guinness Book of Records* as the best-selling author in the world.

She is unique in that she was one and two in the Dalton List of Best Sellers, and one week had four books in the top twenty.

In private life Barbara Cartland, who is a Dame of the Order of St. John of Jerusalem, Chairman of the St. John Council in Hertfordshire and Deputy President of the St. John Ambulance Brigade, has also fought for better conditions and salaries for Midwives and Nurses.

Barbara Cartland is deeply interested in Vitamin Therapy and is President of the British National Association for Health. Her book *The Magic of Honey* has sold throughout the world and is translated into many languages. Her designs "Decorating with Love" are being sold all over the U.S.A., and the National Home Fashions League named her in 1981, "Woman of Achievement."

Barbara Cartland's Romances (a book of cartoons) has been published in Great Britain and the U.S.A., as well as a cookery book, *The Romance of Food*, and *Getting Older, Growing Younger*.